# Khadar
## Fated Dragon Daddies
### Book 3

## Pepper North

Text copyright© 2024 Pepper North
All Rights Reserved

# Author's Note:

The following story is completely fictional. The characters are all over the age of 18 and as adults choose to live their lives in an age play environment.

This is a series of books that can be read in any order. You may, however, choose to read them sequentially to enjoy the characters best. Subsequent books will feature characters that appear in previous novels as well as new faces.

You can contact me on
my Pepper North Facebook pages,
at www.4peppernorth.club
eMail at 4peppernorth@gmail.com
I'm experimenting with Instagram, Twitter, and Tiktok.
Come join me everywhere!

# Prologue

Nestled in the center of a ring of imposing mountains, the village of Wyvern has existed for hundreds of years. Its quaint town center wraps around a square featuring a commanding dragon statue elevated on a block-wide platform for all to admire. The words chiseled into the risers of the stone steps are a mystery to most. Almost all of the ninety-plus commemorative etchings feature the last names of the founding families of the town without explanation. During the prosperity of technological tools, most forgot the old ways.

One female descendant of each founding family has traditionally served as the keeper of knowledge. Passing a huge tome from generation to generation, that woman knows of the pact the original settlers made with the first inhabitants of this land. The agreement between the huge, lethal creatures living in the mountaintops and the struggling, besieged humans sealed the duties for both sides. Promising protection for the people and fated mates for the dragons, this pact has evaporated from the minds of most of the citizens of Wyvern. But the dragons have not forgotten.

When all things powered by technology suddenly ceased to function, the worst features of humanity erupted as people struggled to survive. Once again, the strength and power of the massive beasts who have guarded the city is needed. Revealing themselves once again to the masses, the dragon horde fulfills their promise.

As descendants of those original families are found, mate bonds are forged between dragons and humans. The old ways are essential to the survival of all, and the ancient pact will soar in importance once again. For there are dragons, and they hunt for more than just prey.

Two dragons of the horde have recently discovered their mates in the growing population of Wyvern. Others still search, hoping that each day brings their mate back to their ancestors' home. The stakes are dire for the shifters. Mates create a balance between their human and dragon identities. One teeters on the brink of madness without the companionship of a mate.

# Chapter 1

Loud pounding on the door made Lalani freeze in the doorway to the family room. When it continued, she set the bowl of stale crackers and a few morsels of cheese on a table and crept to the door. Lalani looked over her shoulder to make sure Lettuce was safe on the couch. She could see a hint of green fabric behind the cushions.

"Lalani Quintana! We know you're inside. Open the door immediately. All residents are required to attend the Wyvern gathering."

Her eyes widened in fear before she clenched her jaw in anger as her emotions warred inside her. Like she was going to open her door to hear more threats. Her mother's neighbors had elected themselves to be the wardens of the block. Despite the police telling them she could continue to live in her birth mother's house, they wouldn't stop plotting to make her life as difficult as possible.

When she'd left to go to the big meeting in the square, they'd thrown her suitcase into the street and sealed the door locks with superglue. Thankfully, she had left a window unlocked off the elevated deck. They hadn't discovered that.

The kind gentleman still running the hardware store had changed the front door lock for her. She'd grilled cookies for him with the last of the propane tank.

*Bang. Bang. Bang!*

"Go away. I'm not in the party mood," she yelled, feeling brave with the door between them.

"Lalani Quintana. You are required to attend. Open the door or we will remove it."

They were going to break the door down? What craziness was this? When they struck the door again, making the entire barrier shudder, she rushed forward to unlock it. She couldn't live in a house without a door. Her heart pounded inside her chest as she saw the burly men standing on her doorstep. These guys weren't messing around.

"Lalani Quintana, you will come with us."

One stepped closer. He didn't try to usher her out but reached around her to pick her up. The others parted as he turned to carry her toward a waiting trailer being pulled by a horse. Lalani pushed against his chest, struggling to free herself.

"Please don't make me leave. My neighbors are psycho. They'll break in if I'm not here." She tried to appeal to the man's sympathy.

"Your neighbors are already at the gathering," the man answered without hesitating.

"Please. I can't go like this. Give me five minutes to put some clothes on," she begged as they approached the old-fashioned conveyance.

"Not happening," the man said. "You are the last straggler."

Heat flooded her face as everyone turned to watch them. This was so embarrassing. She couldn't imagine what the other riders thought as she was hauled to the cart. Lalani reminded herself they were there for not following the mandate as well. It didn't help.

He set her feet on the wooden floor of the cart and closed the tailgate. Lalani cowered into the corner as the others confined in the cart looked her over. All were in various states of casual dress. She was the only one in a nightshirt. Lalani wrapped her arms around herself and hunched her shoulders, trying to disguise her lack of a bra.

"Are you okay?" a young man asked.

She nodded.

The others chatted around her. Lalani couldn't make small talk. She could feel herself shaking as stress and embarrassment overwhelmed her. Why hadn't she taken the time to listen to what people told her about the event? The town leaders had even come door to door. Wrapped up in trying to adapt to the new way of life without technology, the loss of her mother, and the threat from next door, Lalani had simply not understood.

The enormous building containing the gathering loomed in front of her. She could see people inside and hear the music and conversations. When the cart stopped, she hung back in the corner as the escorts ushered people in. The same man swooped in and took her arm to tug her out and drag her inside. He deposited her in the middle of the dance floor.

Lalani was horrified to find herself the center of everyone's attention and wished the floor would open and swallow her up. She stared down at her plush slippers. They were the welcome present her mother had given her. She'd wanted Lalani to feel at home. They'd both laughed so hard the first time she'd worn the green slippers. Who would have thought of making dragons fuzzy?

A loud voice announced the last guest had entered, and everyone seemed to look at her with resentment that she had slowed down something. A second announcement followed that the buffet would open shortly. A surge of people, obviously wishing to be first, came toward her, and Lalani panicked, looking around for an exit.

She couldn't escape in any direction. Her pulse raced as people drew closer on all sides. Lalani closed her eyes, expecting to be swept up by the crowd or worse, knocked off her feet and trampled.

A kind female voice told her, "Hey. It's okay. I'm Ciel."

Lalani opened her eyes to see a younger woman standing in front of her. Her smiling violet-colored eyes were simultaneously kind and concerned. An equally friendly woman with shorter hair joined them. The newcomer reached out a hand to touch Lalani's arm softly. Sensing these women would help her, Lalani tried to keep it together.

"I didn't want to come. They made me." She blinked tears away. Her voice was shaky with emotion.

"Everyone is required to be at the gathering. It's okay. You can stay with us," Ciel said, waving a hand at the other woman. "You've got two new friends. This is Aurora."

"Lady Ciel. I have an overdress," an older woman announced from behind Ciel. "I brought this just in case. It will fit over her shirt."

"You are a lifesaver, Abby." Ciel praised the new arrival. "Here. Let me help you."

The three women swarmed around her, forcing the crowd to flow around them. They helped Lalani into a length of material that wrapped around her and tied with a belt in front. It transformed her nightshirt into a dress that covered her.

"Thank you," Lalani whispered.

"We're glad to help. What's your name?" Aurora asked.

"Lalani."

"What a pretty name," Aurora said with a smile.

"Who are those guys?" Lalani asked.

Ciel glanced over her shoulder to see the two large men positioned behind them. "Those are our dragon mates: Drake and Argenis. They're the good guys."

A voice shouted over the hubbub of chatter, announcing that the main buffet was now open. The surrounding crowd surged toward the side of the room, where a delicious aroma emanated. She got jostled by the hungry town's people, and the two women wrapped their arms around her to keep the small group together.

When they were swept away from the dragons, Lalani watched the two shifters force their way through the people. It was obvious they were trying not to hurt anyone but were determined to protect their mates. Someone rammed into them from behind. Lalani and the others struggled to stay on their feet. Off-balance, they fell to their knees. She clung to the women as they all tried to stand to avoid being trampled.

A tremendous roar made everyone freeze. Instinctively, Lalani cowered toward the floor, sure this was the end. A second deep roar combined with the first. Taking advantage of the pause of the crowd's motion, Ciel stood and pulled Lalani and Aurora up. Lalani happened to be looking at Ciel when a third roar echoed with the others. The hair on the back of Lalani's neck stood straight up, alerting her that something important was happening. Ciel's face showed her surprise as she turned toward the source of that third roar. The relief written on her new friend's face changed to joy.

*What is going on?*

Lalani searched for the source of that sound.

"Who was that?" Aurora asked.

"Khadar," Ciel told her with a radiant smile.

"Oh!" Aurora answered, sounding pleased.

"Who's Khadar?" Lalani asked. Ciel simply pointed behind her.

Holding her breath, she pivoted to face him. Lalani gasped as an immensely muscular man walked toward her. He was handsome with beautiful green eyes that held hers captive until she yanked her gaze away to scan the crowd. Lalani noticed his path never wavered. People automatically moved out of his way.

He claimed a spot equally distant from the two men in front, with the women enclosed between them. Before she could whisper a question to Ciel or Aurora, one large shifter ordered everyone back to their original spot and asked Khadar to guard them from the rear.

She didn't have to worry about whether she was invited to go. Aurora and Ciel each took an arm and drew her with the group. Lalani couldn't resist the urge to glance over her shoulder at the man following them. When she found him watching her, she shivered at the feel of his gaze fixed on her —was this how prey felt in the presence of a hunter? Quickly, she focused on the path ahead.

The crowd separated, allowing them safe and easy passage through the crowd. Ciel grabbed the arm of the woman who had clothed her and pulled her into the safe zone. The group reached a raised dais in the room's corner. Lalani stepped up, grateful to have some division from the main floor. Pausing to focus on the Wyvern town folk, she relaxed. The mood of those passing was jovial and excited. There were just so many of them that the massive surge was hard to withstand.

Movement caught her attention, and she watched one large dragon shifter lift Ciel into his arms. He whispered something into her ear, and color flooded her new friend's face. What was he telling her? She turned to check with

Aurora that everything was okay and found herself face to face with Khadar. Unable to stop herself, she scanned his powerful body, marveling how his clothing failed to conceal his chiseled muscles.

"Little One."

She looked up at him, feeling her face heat in embarrassment. *Stop checking him out!*

His eyes flashed green, wiping all thoughts from her mind.

It didn't scare Lalani. In fact, she took a step closer to him. Her mouth rounded in an O of surprise as he lowered himself smoothly to kneel on one leg. He reached out a hand in a silent request for hers. Unable to resist, she placed her palm on his.

When his fingers closed around her hand, she felt a flash of pain and tried to yank her arm back. "Ouch!" she said when he held her hand, trapped.

"I'm sorry, Little One. The discomfort is fleeting. I hope it's better now," he said and squeezed Lalani's fingers lightly before releasing her.

Surprised to find he was correct, she looked at her hand, trying to see what had hurt her. She saw a vague pattern of dots. "What did you do to me?" she asked, moving her hand behind her back.

"It wasn't just me. It's the combination of both of us. I've been searching for you," he shared. "I am Khadar. What is your name?"

*He's been searching for me?* When he looked at her as if he was waiting for an answer, she seized on the last thing she remembered him saying. "I've never met a Khadar before."

"It's ancient, referring to a lush green land. Who are you?"

"I'm Lalani. I know it's a really sexy name for someone like me."

"What do you mean by someone like you?" he asked. She watched his eyebrows draw together in concern, like he didn't know what she meant.

"It's Hawaiian. My dad loved it. It means royal child of heaven. That's a pretty lofty name for someone ordinary." Lalani didn't know why she was still talking. She never said anything—especially not to strangers.

"You are not to speak poorly about yourself." Khadar looked at her sternly, and her heart skipped a beat at his stern tone.

*That shouldn't make me hot.*

Dragging her thoughts back to reality, Lalani didn't argue with him. He was just being nice. There was no way this handsome man would be interested in her, despite his elegant manners in kneeling before her. She'd probably never see Khadar again.

"Sorry to waste your time. I'll let you get back to the celebration," she said quickly and dashed into the crowd, feeling bad that she didn't take time to thank Ciel and Aurora for coming to her aid.

"Wait, Lalani." Khadar's voice followed her.

She looked back to see the concern on his face as he rose and started after her. Lalani ducked around a group of tall men and tried to fade into the crowd. She didn't get very far before pain lanced through her chest. Pressing a hand to her heart, she mentally begged, *Please don't let me be having a heart attack.* It felt like her heart was being torn in two.

Warm arms wrapped around her and pulled Lalani close. Lalani knew his identity without looking but glanced over her shoulder to see Khadar. Her body recognized him by feel alone.

"Princess. You will hurt yourself. The mate bond will demand that we're in close proximity until our mating."

"Our m—mating?" she stuttered.

"That pain you felt. That was the mate bond locking in place. It will continue to strengthen. Look at your hand, Lalani."

Under his watchful eye, she raised her hand. Where previously there had been a scattering of dots, now partial lines appeared. The pattern had grown darker. It was in the vague shape of a winged beast. *A dragon!*

"You're one of them. That's why you are ginormous. No one has muscles on top of muscles like you do," she accused.

"I am one of the dragon protectors of Wyvern," he agreed.

"And those women who were nice to me. They're mated to dragons?"

"Just as you are."

Lalani stared at him, trying to get everything sorted in her head. She took a step away, and he relaxed his hold. Instantly, she missed the contact with his hard body. Why did she want to rub her hands all over him? She felt more turned on by simply standing by this man than she had during the few disastrous dates she'd forced herself to go on in the past. Struggling to process all the emotions and control her physical reactions, Lalani could only shake her head in disbelief.

"You are my mate," he repeated.

"But, why me?"

"I cannot answer that. Additionally, I don't know why you're mated to me and not to one of the other dragons," Khadar told her, seeming honest.

"Are you going to eat me?" she asked.

"I will not harm you."

Lalani noticed he switched her words. *Deliberately?* Her

confused brain sparked with a visual image of herself stretched out on her back with her legs draped over his shoulders. She looked up at him, reacting to that mental picture.

"Our mating will be glorious, Lalani."

Her face flamed hot at his confident statement. "Can you read my mind?" she whispered.

"Your face is very expressive, Princess. I didn't need to eavesdrop on your thoughts."

"Why are you calling me princess?"

"Royal child of the heavens. That sounds like a princess to me. I think it fits you well."

"Oh."

*He actually thinks I'm a princess. How in the world is this happening? It's impossible to deny our connection. The mating bond. Between me and a dragon shifter. A drop-dead gorgeous dragon shifter who looks at me as if I were a snack he wanted to devour.*

"I like whatever you're thinking. Unfortunately, I'll have to wait to find out the details."

## Chapter 2

"Khadar, can I just tell your mate she's going to be okay?" Aurora asked, hovering a few steps away.

"Thank you, Lady Aurora, for your concern about my mate."

"It's hard to understand at first. I wish our families had shared the information more than handing down that old book," Aurora told him with a disgruntled expression.

"What does my family have to do with this?" Lalani asked as Ciel came to join them.

"Did you ever hear the legend of the town?" Ciel asked.

"No. I didn't grow up here. My adoptive parents lived a few hundred miles from Wyvern. They always bragged about how they'd chosen me. Of course, I'd wondered about my birth parents. When I found my birth mother lived here and was willing to meet me, I left my job and came to visit. Unfortunately, she and her husband were killed in a car accident a few days after I arrived. My adoptive parents both passed a few years ago."

"I'm so sorry, Lalani," Aurora said with tears in her eyes. "Do you have any brothers or sisters?"

"No. I'm the only one left now."

Khadar wiped a tear from his mate's cheek and drew her closer so her side rested against him. The tension eased from her body as she relaxed against him.

"I can't imagine what it feels like to be completely alone. I'm glad Khadar found you. You're part of our family now," Ciel assured her.

He smiled fondly at the gold and silver dragon's mates. The women had dressed and protected his mate. He would be eternally thankful.

Lalani's stomach growled ferociously, and she slapped a hand over her abdomen to muffle it. "Sorry!"

"I am not taking care of you as I should, Lalani. Come. We will get you something to eat," Khadar declared.

Intertwining his fingers with hers, Khadar led her through the crowd past all those standing in line to reach the buffet. His mate tugged at his hand, resisting him.

"Hey! You can't jump past all of us in line," an angry male voice announced.

Khadar turned and speared him with a look, allowing him to see a bit of his dragon shining through his eyes. The crowd glared angrily at the protester.

Backpedaling, the man apologized, "Oh. Sorry. Dragons first."

"Khadar, it's okay. I don't need to eat," Lalani whispered as she tried to tug him away.

"No. He spoke without knowing who... the dragon was," a female organizer of the gathering said. "We owe our lives to those who protect Wyvern. Of course, they do not need to stand in line. Without Khadar, the gardens would not have been completed for a long time. Please, Sir Dragon, take your mate to the front."

A chorus of "yes" and "he can take my place" echoed

through the crowd. Forcing his annoyance away to focus on his mate, Khadar wrapped his arm around Lalani and picked her up to carry her the last few feet to the front. After setting her feet gently on the floor, he took a plate and ushered her through the buffet, heaping her plate with anything she indicated she liked.

"I can't eat all that, Khadar."

"You will enjoy anything you wish."

"I don't want the food to go to waste," she whispered.

"It won't. Anything else?" he asked.

"Good gracious, no."

"Let's return to the others. Look. They are behind us."

The dais was empty in the corner. Khadar claimed a large chair, setting the plate on a nearby table. He lifted Lalani from her feet and balanced her on his thick thigh. Immediately, she tried to scoot off.

"Stay here, Lalani. Are you uncomfortable?"

"I can't sit on your lap," she hissed, looking around to see if anyone was watching.

"No one cares, Princess. You are safe here, and there are seats for the others."

Lalani counted the chairs. He was right. She didn't want her new friends to have to stand—or the immense shifters. They weren't people to piss off. Not that they had done anything scary. They had protected her even before she'd been claimed by Khadar as his mate.

A fork appeared in front of her mouth, and she accepted the bite automatically before realizing he was feeding her.

"I can do it," she stated firmly and reached for the fork.

"Not happening."

When he lifted another tempting morsel to her lips, Lalani closed her mouth tightly and shook her head. "Uh-uh."

"Behavior like this will earn you a spanking in the future. This is your only warning."

The stern glint in his green eyes made her relent. He was not kidding. As she chewed, he added, "You are hungry. Let me take care of you. Especially now. I'm fighting the urge to rampage this gathering."

She swallowed and asked, "Why?"

"They dragged you here in your night attire and scared you."

"That was frightening. I didn't understand what was happening and why. It's always embarrassing to be undressed in front of others."

"The men saw you without clothing?" Khadar roared possessively. Every fiber of his being vibrated around her.

"No. It wasn't like that," she rushed to assure him, inwardly tickled that he was so protective. "I was in my nightshirt. I wasn't naked."

The tension in his body eased against her. Well, grew not as alert. Did he ever completely relax?

"Eat."

She accepted another bite, watching his face. Khadar divided his time between looking at her and scoping out the surrounding for threats. "Are you afraid of them?" she asked.

"Of the humans?" he asked in indignation.

"One puff of flames and the building is toast," Ciel said in a teasing tone that didn't detract from the truth of that statement.

Argenis sat next to Khadar and scooped Ciel up to perch on his lap as well. Lalani noticed Ciel didn't make any move to resist. It was as if she did this often.

"Eat, Little One. You are safe here," Khadar said softly against her ear.

Drake and Aurora joined them and occupied the same chair as well. That left one empty chair. Were there any more dragons with mates?

A movement caught her attention. Drake sat up even straighter, if that was possible. His nod toward the door made the other shifters focus that way immediately. They reacted as well, as if they were on guard.

"Is everything okay?" Lalani whispered.

"It's Keres. He's the black dragon. He's checking for his mate. Fingers crossed he finds her," Aurora said softly.

Keres was harshly handsome. His face was as chiseled as the others, but he seemed more... relentless?

When he turned to look at them gathered on the dais, Lalani huddled against Khadar, instinctively knowing he would ensure her safety. Khadar's arm tightened around her. "You are fine, Princess."

The conversation between the shifters and their mates continued, but Lalani noticed everyone kept Keres in view. When he'd circled the room twice with forays into the side rooms and along the buffet line, Aurora swore, "Damn."

"Language, Little One," Drake warned.

Lalani was glad she wasn't the scolded woman.

"He didn't find his mate, did he?" Ciel whispered.

"I did not," Keres said as he approached. "My congratulations, Khadar, for locating yours. She is lovely."

"Do not scare my mate, Keres. It will not bode well for you," Khadar growled.

The air seemed to heat as Keres glared back at Khadar. Lalani didn't dare move. It seemed like the situation could ignite at any second. The atmosphere felt electric, pricking over her skin.

"Are you a dragon?" a coquettish voice asked.

Lalani stared at the woman who had dared approach before rolling her eyes at the sight of the bane of her existence. Barbie Ann Peterson, her next-door neighbor who'd caused so many problems.

Keres simply glared down at her in exasperation. He didn't reply but glanced back at the others. "Luck does not seem to favor me. Maybe next time."

He turned to leave, and the eager woman trailed behind him, "Hi. I'm Barbie. What's your name?"

Keres never paused as he strode toward the exit.

"Hey. You have crappy manners. I'm just trying to take pity on you," Barbie spat after him.

Keres wheeled, eyes glowing black with anger. "I need no one's pity, newcomer. Your family will never produce a mate. Don't waste our time."

A hush fell over the room. Everyone was watching the interaction. The shocked look on Barbie's face almost made having to hide inside her mother's house worthwhile. Almost. Processing through his words, Lalani realized Keres had just dismissed not only Barbie but her entire family as inconsequential.

"Dragons obviously have extremely poor taste," Barbie announced to the silent crowd who turned to look at the mates on the dais.

Lalani knew she was targeting her with that dig. She regretted that Aurora and Ciel were included in the negative comment. Putting on a brave face, Lalani didn't want Barbie to know her barb had affected her.

The three seated dragons bristled. Ciel pressed a hand to Drake's chest and corrected her, "Being a dragon's mate is a true honor and should not be cause for resentment."

Barbie shrugged that comment off and returned to her seat. The hubbub of voices rekindled immediately.

"Could she be more unpleasant? Keres just became my favorite shifter," Ciel joked. The immediate growl from the dragon holding her made her backpedal. "You're my mate not simply a shifter, Daddy."

"I'd hope so," Argenis growled, obviously having not forgotten her statement.

Did Ciel call the shifter Daddy?

Flashes of erotic scenes ricocheted through Lalani's mind. She knew there were Daddy books, but she'd always preferred the illicit videos and drawings she'd found on the internet. Her favorite fantasies about a powerful male who'd take care of everything and discipline her when she didn't follow his rules were difficult to locate, but with determination, she'd found some good ones. Really enticing ones. Now that the internet had ceased to exist, all that was gone.

She peeked up at Khadar, who watched her carefully. He lifted a fork to tempt her with more food.

"I'm not hungry anymore." Sadly, she noticed a heap still remained on the plate. Barbie Ann was the best diet plan. Who could eat after all that negativity? She hated to waste food when it was more difficult to obtain and prepare. An image of the almost empty peanut butter jar waiting for her at home popped into her mind.

"We'll work on it together," he suggested and ate the bite himself. Wooing her with the choicest selections, Khadar tempted her from time to time to enjoy more as he devoured the food on the plate.

Lalani watched the other shifters do the same. How much could these men consume?

"Dragons," Aurora explained when Lalani looked at her in disbelief.

"Why do I believe that's the answer for everything?" Lalani said without thinking.

Aurora and Ciel laughed and nodded. "You've already figured that out. It took us a week or so."

When the plate was empty, Lalani rested her head against Khadar's chest. She was so tired. For the first moment in a long time, she felt safe. Closing her eyes, she listened to the gathering around her.

# Chapter 3

Feeling his mate relax into sleep against him made Khadar treasure her even more. In a short period, he'd already discovered she did not trust easily. He suspected she didn't interact frequently with others but kept to herself.

She had, however, talked easily with the other mates. This was reassuring because he did not wish for her to be lonely. The mates of this present day seemed different—more social. Spending time with others seemed important. He had come across Aurora and Ciel with Drake and Argenis supervising. Khadar set a mental reminder to invite the two women over to interact with Lalani. He didn't want her to be as isolated as he suspected she'd been.

He didn't like that the residents of Wyvern had dragged her to the gathering. But what if she had never left her house? He would not have found her.

The dragons without mates flashed into his head. The blue, bronze, red, and black dragons still searched for their mates. He'd seen each walk through the assembled crowd as they rotated off guard duty and then leave alone. Of all of them, Keres had gone the longest without a mate. His mind was still clear, but his temperament was turning as black as his dragon form.

The dragons would have to talk about him soon. Khadar shook that thought from his mind. That conversation would have to occur in the future but not now. Tonight was the night to celebrate.

"I will take Lalani home now," he told the others and stood with his mate cradled in his arms. Her closeness eased the possessive need inside him.

"We will join you in flight," Drake decreed. Argenis rose to his feet as well. They scooped their protesting mates up in their arms and walked to the exit.

Khadar followed the path they'd created through the villagers. To his surprise, many Wyvern dwellers called their congratulations and good wishes. The stories of life outside their ring of mountains were difficult to hear. Lawlessness and selfishness ruled. The dragons prevented the threat of vandals and murderers attacking to take everything. The townspeople worked together to help one another survive and establish a life free of worry for food, clean water, and medical care. Bad apples existed, but those were dealt with harshly. The banished could never return.

Khadar reached a cleared area apart from the others. He brushed his fingers through her short, thick hair. "Lalani. Princess. It's time to get up."

"I don't want to, Daddy."

His heart skipped a beat when she called him that name, but he tamped down his excitement. She must think she was talking to her father.

"Lalani. You must wake up for the flight back to my lands. If you want to sleep, I'll carry you in my claw."

"That doesn't sound like a good idea," she said, rubbing

her eyes to try and wake up. "I can walk to my house from here. It's a few blocks. Ten minutes max."

Khadar set her feet on the ground but kept his arms around her for support. "You do not live at your mother's anymore, Princess. Your place is with me."

"You don't understand. Barbie and her family have done everything to drive me from my mom's home. I want to stay there to learn more about her—my mother, not Barbie. If I leave, I may never get back inside."

Worry lines appeared on her face. She was more upset than she'd been at the gathering. Instantly, he rethought his plan. "That will not happen. Show me where the house is," Khadar requested, scooping her up in his arms.

"I can walk."

"You are tired. We will deal with this neighbor problem first, only because you will not sleep well if it is not handled."

As they approached, Khadar heard whispers in the night breeze. Something was definitely afoot.

"Take the last of the food. She'll have to leave."

He recognized that voice. Anger brewed inside him.

"They're in there. Lights are bouncing around inside," Lalani said as she struggled to free herself from his arms.

"I will set you down, but you will need to let me enter first, Lalani. Promise?"

"There's something important in there. I have to save him."

"What, Lalani?"

She hesitated. "Can you just believe that I need to protect my belongings?"

"For the moment, yes. Will you have faith in me? I will deal with these neighbors."

A long second passed, and she nodded. Khadar didn't trust that assurance at all. On guard, he stood her next to him.

The moment her feet touched the grass, she was off. Having anticipated her flight, Khadar wrapped his hands around her upper arms and stopped her.

"You will be punished for lying, mate," he said softly. "Do I tie your body to mine with my belt or will you stay behind me?"

"Behind," she chose. "Can we get in there, please?"

Khadar walked forward, entered through the entrance, and roared, "Peterson clan. Come immediately to the front door."

Whispers abounded as they debated whether to comply or refuse.

"Now. You have five seconds before I turn into a dragon and set your house on fire."

"You can't do that!" Barbie appeared in the doorway flanked by two men—one younger and one older.

"Her brother and father," Lalani whispered, peeking around his wide frame.

"This is not your house. Nor are you the warden of it. Leave and never return," Khadar demanded.

They started forward to the door, dragging almost empty trash bags behind them.

"Drop everything here," Khadar informed them. Lalani gripped his arm tightly as she peered around him.

"Oh, we brought this stuff," the brother insisted.

"Then it became Lalani's the moment you entered her house without permission," Khadar told him.

After a moment's hesitation, they dropped the sacks.

Khadar stepped to the side, keeping Lalani shielded, to allow them to exit. When they were clear, he told her, "Let me enter first in case of traps."

When they were safely inside, he instructed, "Go get whatever was so important."

She ran toward the couch and threw the pillows the robbers had knocked around in all directions. "Lettuce," she whispered, grabbing a worn, plush item and hugging it to her heart. "I'm so glad you're okay."

"Would you introduce me, Lalani?" he requested.

"This is Lettuce. He's my oldest friend. I've had him since I was a baby."

As he watched, Lalani sheepishly held out a battered green dragon. "I didn't know it when I was little, but Lettuce was a gift from my birth mom when I was adopted. She told me she'd visited a toy store here in Wyvern to get me a teddy bear, but Lettuce caught her eye."

"I am glad to meet you, Lettuce. I can see how important you are to Lalani." Khadar tried to control his elation at seeing the stuffie. It was so well loved. And green, of course.

"I think he's happy too," she said with a small smile before commenting on the stuffie's name. "Lettuce is a silly name, but it suits him."

"I believe it is a perfectly appropriate name for a green dragon. I bet you'll need to come home with us."

"I can't go without him."

"Of course you can't," Khadar agreed before looking at the sacks in the entryway. "Let's get all this put back away."

It didn't take long for Lalani to store the squished butter stick, a few withered potatoes and carrots, and the almost empty peanut butter jar. The additional things in the bags made Khadar's blood boil. Knives, jewelry, and personal items that had become so needed: soap, shampoo, and toilet paper.

His gaze lingered on the knives. They had deliberately taken the only weapons Lalani had to defend herself. The vein at his temple throbbed with outrage. Those people were the worst kind of bullies.

He sent a mental call to Keres.

*Bring a transport cage to my location.*

"Go pack a suitcase, Lalani, for you and Lettuce. You will return to my home with me."

"But they'll come back the minute you leave."

"They will not," Khadar assured her and followed her through the house to pick up the few items she'd unpacked over the time she'd lived there.

"Remain here on your front steps. That should be close enough for the mate bond."

"O—Okay."

Khadar walked outside and over to the neighboring house. Taking hold of their door, he ripped it off the hinges.

The father shot at him.

Khadar dodged the bullet, enraged. His dragon was close to assuming control, and his eyes were blazing green.

"You have two minutes to gather anything precious you wish to take with you. Any further aggression will result in the loss of that privilege," Khadar growled.

"You don't have the right to tell us that," Barbie said, stepping next to her father.

"You cannot endanger a dragon's mate. Consider yourself lucky to be alive."

Khadar stepped back into the open space in front of the house and released the beast inside him. Immediately, that area became much smaller as his dragon form filled it. He treasured Lalani's gasp of amazement while trying to tune out the squeal Barbie let out as she fled into her house.

Neighbors gathered in the street. Khadar was not surprised when no one came to the Petersons' defense. Obviously, Lalani had not been the only one they'd targeted.

The sound of wings approached, and he shifted away from the building. *Put it against the door.*

Keres, almost invisible in the night sky, hovered. He set the cage with its waist-high railings against the Peterson house and retreated.

Khadar blew a blast of smoke into the house.

"The house is on fire. Get out!" Barbie's voice screeched.

The three came running from their home with empty hands. Jumping over the railing, they attempted to flee through the other side, but Keres immediately lifted the cage off the ground as Khadar's smoking snout kept them from escaping. Barbie's father pulled his gun from the back of his pants. Before he could shoot, Khadar melted the metal with a torrent of flames that set the sleeve of the younger man on fire as it blazed in a narrow path. While the young man frantically batted at the material, Keres soared upward with the cage trapped in his claws. A flaming shirt wafted down from above to smolder at Khadar's feet. He stomped it out with one massive foot.

Spontaneous applause came from the assembled neighbors as Keres's voice sounded in his head.

*Drop them out of town?*

Khadar confirmed the black dragon's assumption. With the crunch of bones breaking and knitting back together, he shifted back into human form. Turning, he addressed the crowd. "They will not return. Take anything you need from this house but share with your neighbors. Leave the residence next door untouched."

"We'll keep an eye on it, Khadar," a familiar voice called. "I promise, Lalani.

Making eye contact, Khadar realized the man who spoke was the leader of his gardening crews. Khadar nodded his thanks, glancing at his mate who silently watched a safe distance away.

"I'll finally get my favorite hammer back," a male crowed

as he ran toward the open doorway. Others followed him, calling out things the Petersons had claimed as their own. No one would miss that family.

Khadar shook his head as he walked back to where Lalani stood with her suitcase and her stuffie clutched tightly to her chest.

"Are you ready to go to my house?" he asked.

"I thought this would be a good place to stay," she answered sadly before darting forward into his arms.

He wrapped his arms around Lalani, holding her close. "Your next home will be your last, Princess."

"Can we go there now? Is it far?"

He was pleased her voice had lost most of the frightened tone. "It is difficult to see at night. My lands encompass one of the mountains that encircle Wyvern."

"Not the slopes with all the trees and grasses planted in a pattern that looks like diamonds."

"Emeralds," he corrected. "You are correct. My team of gardeners has created the effect of stones joined together. Everything is green. Emeralds."

"Do diamonds come in green?" She got the words out before an enormous yawn cracked her jaw.

A wave of tenderness filled him. He needed to care for his mate. "Let's talk about this later. You need to be in bed."

"You're going to fly me there?" she asked.

"Yes, Princess. You choose. I'm going to walk a few feet away and allow my dragon to come out and greet you. Then you may lie on the grass, and I will pick you up. Or you can climb on my scales and hold onto my neck."

"I will ride on your back."

"Step on my front leg," he recommended.

"Is there a saddle or a bridle?"

"I am not a horse, Princess. You will find a comfortable

place to stretch out with your arms around my neck. Tuck Lettuce inside your bodice to keep him safe."

"Sorry," she whispered.

"It was an honest question. You are allowed to ask me anything," Khadar told her softly. "Stand back, and I will change."

This time, as his dragon formed, the noise she made seemed less surprised and more amazed. Khadar could live with that. It was pretty damn special to see the transformation. The feeling of freedom and power still elated him each time. He bent down to make it easier for her to climb into position. The feel of her body against his scales was less noticeable but still precious. When she settled with her arms around him, he thought to her.

*Hold on, Princess.*

Launching into the air, he celebrated her excitement and awe at being carried up into the night sky. His mate was brave. And quick-witted. It didn't take long for her to process that if he could talk to her, she might be able to answer.

*You can read my thoughts?*

*Only when you concentrate on sending a message to me. At some point, we may decide to open the lines of conversation fully.*

*No way!* drifted to him, and he knew she hadn't meant for him to hear that response. He released a snort of laughter and felt her cringe.

*Are you going to breathe fire?*

*No, Princess. Even if I did, I would not put you in danger. Your safety is more important than mine.*

*What will happen to Barbie?*

*I don't care. Her family was not from Wyvern, nor were they willing to contribute positively to life here. Do not think of them again.*

A jumble of emotions answered that decree.

*Try not to worry about them, Princess.*

*Okay.*

Frustrated that he couldn't erase all her worries and the pain from the last weeks, Khadar chose to concentrate on flying smoothly. He would make this first trip as easy on his mate as he could.

# Chapter 4

Lalani blinked wearily as she slid down from the scaled back that had carried her out of town and to the top of the green mountain. The power of the massive body below her made her feel vulnerable, but Khadar had treated her only with kindness.

After retrieving Lettuce from the safe place wrapped inside the material of her dress, she looked around. In the darkness, she couldn't see very much. After leaving the lights of the city, she hadn't been able to see anything below. Exhaustion muted her disappointment. Maybe he'd take her flying again when it was light. He had landed in a clearing before a large building.

She watched closely as he shifted into human form but just saw a shimmer. Rubbing her eyes, she tried looking again.

"Come on, Princess."

Taking her hand, he guided her toward the building. She resisted. Why were they visiting a museum or a castle? "I thought we were going to your house."

"This is our home, Lalani. Come inside. It's time for you to be in bed."

"You live here?" She rubbed her eyes again.

"*We* live here."

When she stumbled on the stairs, he lifted her into his arms and carried her to the entrance. A woman opened the door for them, holding two lanterns.

"Welcome back, sir. Do you need food?"

"No, thank you, Patricia. My mate only needs to sleep now. I will introduce her to the staff tomorrow." He took a lantern before turning toward one darkened hallway.

"Hi, Patricia," Lalani said drowsily as he walked away.

"Welcome, miss. Sleep well. And congratulations to you both."

"She's nice," Lalani whispered, letting her heavy eyelids rest.

"Yes, Little One."

"Where am I sleeping?"

"With me."

That seemed to make sense. She enjoyed being close to him. Lalani inhaled, and the corners of her mouth turned up slightly. His scent was yummy—male and something more. Dragon. Sexy dragon.

"Sexy dragon?" Khadar asked with a lilt of humor in his voice, leading her through a sumptuous bedroom she hardly had a chance to see and into an enormous bathroom.

"I didn't mean to say that aloud," she mumbled, her face heating with embarrassment.

"I see." He halted next to a door and added, "I'm going to stand you here by the toilet."

"Oh! Good idea. I need to go," she admitted. Once on her feet, she wobbled, trying to maintain her balance.

"Here, Princess. Let's set Lettuce on the vanity. He can

watch to make sure you're okay," Khadar suggested as he steadied her. His ease in supporting her underlined their differences. Even shifting and flying here hadn't seemed to impact his strength.

When her hands were free, Khadar supported her as he removed the wrap dress. After sniffing, he growled.

"Do I stink?" she asked, mesmerized by how his eyes glowed slightly green in the lantern's light. How precise were his senses?

"You, never. This nightshirt holds the scent of the men who took you to the gathering. It has to go. My dragon doesn't like the scent of other males on you. He's territorial."

"Oh!" She stared up at him, not sure what she should say. His possessiveness felt... good. Amazingly good.

"Go potty," he ordered.

Thankfully, the toilet was a separate area. Still, she was aware of his presence at the wall. Finishing, she felt like the absolute last of her energy disappeared as she joined him.

"I'm too tired to change."

"I know, Princess."

He picked up Lalani before snagging the lantern and Lettuce from the vanity. She loved that he tucked Lettuce in her arms safely as if he were the most precious of possessions. Khadar carried her back into the vast bedroom where she spotted a bed larger than she'd ever seen. It looked deliciously decadent. She wanted to dive in and sleep for a week.

Khadar stopped to drop off the lantern and grab a T-shirt from a drawer. When he stood her at the edge of the bed, she turned to crawl toward the pillows. Khadar thwarted that attempt and held her in place.

Lalani turned to glare at him.

"Let me set Lettuce on a pillow. He's tired," Khadar said and accomplished the task when she reluctantly offered the stuffie to him. With that completed, he pulled her T-shirt over her head and replaced it with a fresh one.

Had he just seen her naked?

She looked up at him. His face was drawn, and a muscle twitched on his cheek. Concerned, she scanned his body to see if he was in pain. Maybe he shouldn't carry her around. When her gaze glanced over his flat stomach, her eyes fixed on something else. A thick erection tented his slacks. Even tired, she automatically reached up to touch it. The display of arousal made her clench her thighs together as the desire she'd tried to ignore flamed hotter.

"You're killing me, mate. But I can control the mating urge long enough for you to sleep. Fair warning. All bets are off when you wake. Come. Let me put you to bed."

Her brain couldn't come up with a snappy answer. She simply wrapped her arms around his neck as he scooped her up. A second later, Khadar tucked Lalani into the softest, crispest sheets she'd ever felt. Closing her eyes, the last snapshot her brain pictured was the view of Khadar taking off his shirt.

"Mmm." Lalani was having the best dream. She rubbed the slightly furry, warm surface below her and inhaled the best scent. "Better than apple pie."

"Are you hungry, mate?"

Her eyes flashed open, and Lalani pushed herself away from the hard body she'd obviously slept on. "Khadar?" She tried to ignore how sexy he looked sleep-tousled and relaxed.

"I hope you don't rest on any other dragons," he teased.

"I'm sorry," she said, trying to slide off his body. How long had she draped herself over him? She shook her head, slightly rebuking herself for seeking out the object of the wanton dreams that still sizzled in her mind.

His arms tightened around her. "Princess, you can't flee from me. We are bonded now."

"I'm not used to being so close to anyone," she whispered, looking down at his bare chest below her. "You know... Sitting on someone's lap or sleeping on top of them."

"I like having you in my arms. Are you uncomfortable?"

"Umm. No." She dared to answer truthfully.

"Good. You look like you feel better."

Lalani nodded. She studied his handsome face for a couple of seconds before she hesitantly asked, "Did I lay on you all night? Where's Lettuce?"

"I enjoyed having you close. Lettuce climbed up on the headboard to keep guard." Khadar pointed to the stuffie above them before asking, "How long has it been since you slept, Lalani?"

"Really slept? Not just napped for a few hours?" When he nodded, she continued, "Since my birth mother was killed. I haven't rested well since. I've been going through her things."

"It's sad you didn't get to spend more time together. I am glad to have found you. Your journey to Wyvern to meet her brought you to me."

"I don't understand what's happening here," Lalani said, waving her fingers back and forth between them. "It feels special."

His slow smile whisked away the lingering sadness and helped her focus on the feelings she seemed to have when he was around. The heat flared deep within her. Daringly, she scooted up a bit and pressed her mouth against his. Instantly, that flame burnt hotter. His fingers glided through her sleep-tangled hair, and he tugged slightly at her scalp.

When she gasped at the hint of pain, he explored her mouth.

Loving his control, Lalani tangled her tongue with his and received her reward. That hand tightened in her hair, tilting her head slightly to the perfect angle. Khadar held her in place as he took complete control of the kiss. The tinge of pain wiped all thoughts from her mind and forced her to be fully present here and now.

His other hand stroked down her back, caressing her tight muscles. She arched her body slightly into his touch to encourage him. When he brushed the side swell of her breast, Lalani couldn't believe how sensitive she was. His touch was electric.

Khadar lowered his mouth from hers to press a passionate kiss to her neck. The sizzle zinged all the way to her pelvis. *How can one kiss make me wet?* She didn't know and didn't care. Lalani waited for the next sensation he would deliver.

"I need to see you, Princess," he growled against her skin before biting her shoulder. He stroked his hands over her rounded bottom.

Distracted by his arousing touch, she missed his fingers sliding her T-shirt over her hips. Cool air wafted over her skin when he sat up. He effortlessly lifted them both to a sitting position as he stripped off the borrowed shirt.

"Oh!" Lalani automatically pulled her hands from his broad shoulders to cover her breasts.

"No, mate. No hiding from Daddy."

He moved her hands behind her back. Holding them with one hand, he pulled her wrists downward, making her arch toward him. He scanned her body. His expression hardened and became... hungry.

"Princess..."

He caressed a line down the side of her body, just as he

had before. The next brushed over her bare skin. His touch electrified her. When he cupped her breast, she shivered from the sensation of his fingers caressing her curves. When he pinched her nipple slightly, she moaned.

"I know, mate. I feel it too."

He lifted his hips to grind his erection against her. Instantly, Lalani responded, wiggling closer to him. This time, she wasn't the only one who groaned.

With a flick of his wrist, the covers landed at the bottom of the bed. Khadar wrapped his arms around her, and Lalani's world whirled as he quickly rotated their bodies so she was under him, releasing her hands. She immediately grabbed his broad shoulders to hold on.

She stared up into his eyes, struggling to think coherently. Her brain didn't seem to be functioning with the onslaught of desire that overwhelmed it.

In a display of athleticism, Khadar rose to kneel between her legs. Lalani ogled his chiseled body without shame. Male beauty like that needed to be admired.

Khadar ripped away the thin pants he'd worn to bed and tossed the scraps over the side of the mattress. Lalani swallowed hard at her first sight of his cock. It was thick and long, and she couldn't imagine how that would fill her. Khadar widened his knees, spreading her thighs to allow him to settle himself flush against her.

The feel of his cock gliding across her pussy made her juices gush. The sensation was totally beyond her comprehension. If he didn't kill her with that thing, it was going to be amazing.

"I will only kill you with pleasure, Little One."

"Khadar, I don't think this is going to work."

"Daddy, Princess."

"Daddy?" She struggled to follow his logic as he moved against her.

"Call me Daddy."

Her gaze locked with his. "Daddy?" Surely, he didn't mean that name with all the connotations of a Daddy Dom. His green eyes blazed once again, and she felt like he could see into the secret places in her mind.

"Yes, Little One. Daddy."

"Daddy," she breathed, denying him nothing.

Cupping one of her breasts, he leaned down to capture her nipple in his lips. The brush of his beard and mustache on her tender flesh added extra sensations as he tasted her ruby-colored tip. He sucked it gently in his mouth and swirled his tongue around the taut peak. She gripped his shoulders, trying not to moan. The slickness between her thighs grew, and she ground herself against him. He drew his mouth back, increasing the pressure, and released his target with an audible pop.

"Always let me hear your sounds, Princess. I'll think I'm doing something wrong."

"That's not possible" popped out of her mouth before she could stop it.

His low chuckle fueled the fire inside her. See! He could even make that sexy.

"I'm glad you believe that. I want to hear what excites you, Lalani." The second part was a definite order. She nodded quickly and closed her eyes. "Good girl."

Lalani didn't want him to know how much he turned her on. She'd never felt so exposed.

"Eyes on mine, Princess."

"Don't I get any privacy?" she demanded.

"None, Little One."

His mouth captured hers, and he kissed her deeply. She was panting when he lifted his lips and clung to him for stability. He captured her gaze before tracing his fingers up the inside of her thigh. It seemed so intimate to have him see how much his touch affected her.

Khadar eased his pelvis away from her to caress her. Gliding through her wetness, he traced her inner labia before brushing across her clit—so lightly that she lifted her hips, trying to get more direct contact. She could see her growing need reflected in his eyes. Their connection was so intimate. It was also hotter than hell. She could see his need for her as well.

She slid one hand from his shoulder to his chest and explored the grooves of his muscles. They led her on a twisting path straight toward his...

He hauled her wrists up above her, pinning them to the pillows. He tethered her arms in place with one hand. "No touching, Princess. You don't have permission."

"Permission?" she repeated, tugging to test how secure his grip was. There was no way she could evade that iron-clad control. Lalani wanted to caress him, but being restrained was hot. Craving him, she lifted her pelvis to press against the hand that had returned to explore her pussy.

"Look at me," he required.

When her gaze fused with his, it felt like he could see inside her. When Khadar slid two fingers into her tight channel, she struggled to keep her eyes from rolling back into her head. Those digits brushed past a thousand nerve endings, making her more sensitive than she imagined possible. If this was his hand, how would his cock fill her?

"Good girls get rewards, Lalani. You want to be a good girl, don't you?"

She nodded without losing eye contact. A question popped into her mind. "What do bad girls get?"

"Bad girls receive what they need."

She didn't ask for clarification. The ominous tone told her she'd hate and love any punishment he would dole out.

"Please" escaped from her mouth.

"You've asked so nicely." His fingers stretched her, continuing to push her arousal higher with a combination of sensuality and a hint of pain.

When his digits slid from her body, she looked down to see her juices dripping from his fingertips.

"I think I need a taste," he said. Khadar raised his hand to his mouth and licked her juices from his skin. "Delicious. Here, try your nectar." He held a fingertip at her lips.

Lalani opened her mouth and extended her tongue tentatively. The flavor was so hedonistic she couldn't resist, and she wrapped her lips around the digit. Swirling her tongue around his finger, she tried to imagine what it would be like to taste his cock. She sucked on it, and his eyelids lowered to half-mast as a deep groan emerged from his throat.

He drew his hand away from her mouth and shifted onto his knees to loom over her. After fitting himself against her, he recaptured her gaze. "Now, mate."

His cock surged into her. Whatever she expected was blown away by the sensation of his thick erection filling her. Readied by his touch, her body adjusted to his dominance. When the pressure swelled to the brink of pain, Lalani bit her lip. Khadar leaned down to kiss her, nudging her teeth away with his tongue before deepening the exchange. As his mouth seduced her, he withdrew slightly before pushing forward again. This time, she relaxed around him, allowing him fully inside. She could feel him brushing against her womb, setting off sensations she didn't know existed.

He paused, allowing her to adjust to his invasion. The slight burn of the stretch only fueled her desire. She kissed him back with excitement escalating inside her body, feeling every millimeter of his body in and over her. He held most of his weight on one forearm to keep from crushing her, but Lalani loved being pinned under him.

Khadar pushed forward a scant inch more to grind his pelvis against her clit. Her body hovered on the edge of pleasure for a fraction of a second before she exploded.

"Ahhh!"

Lalani struggled to process all the emotions and pleasure that cascaded over her. Her connection with Khadar deepened, blending with the sensations of her orgasm. *Daddy! I need to touch you!*

Instantly, he released his hold. She reached desperately for him. Her fingernails dug into the muscles of his powerful shoulders as she ground herself against him, drawing all the delight from her climax.

A brush to her cheek brought her back to focus on him. She took in the hungry need mingled with concern on Khadar's face. Forcing her fingers to relax, she lifted one hand to cup his face.

*The mate bond has fully snapped into place. Are you okay?*

She nodded. *I can sense you in my head.*

*Just wait.*

Khadar withdrew and pressed forward in a slow, controlled thrust. Lalani gasped at the sensations gathering once again inside her. This time, she could feel an avalanche of pleasure. Is this what sex was like for him? The tight grip of her slick walls against his throbbing cock combined with the sensation of his shaft rubbing across all those responsive spots inside her.

*Princess?*

*Move, damn it.*

His deep chuckle echoed in her head as well as in her ears. Without hesitating, Khadar complied. His warm mouth pressed kisses over her skin as they moved together.

His scent mingled with hers as their bodies heated the room. She licked his shoulder, making him groan as she savored his taste. Lalani loved how he experimented with different angles and strokes, searching for whatever brought her the most pleasure.

She ground herself against his cock and tightened her muscles around him, trying to return the attention he lavished on her.

"Touch me, Princess," he growled.

Lalani had fought to follow his mandates. Now, with permission, she explored his powerful torso and back. The feel of the strength corded into each inch of his form was beyond alluring. She tried to memorize every bulge and dip of his muscles, knowing it would take a lifetime to appreciate him completely—especially as he distracted her with such pleasure.

Each time her body hesitated on the edge of a climax, he drove her over that last barrier to pleasure. He dominated her not only physically but mentally with such sensuality. She'd never be the same.

When she screamed his name, Khadar corrected her as he pounded into her body.

*Daddy.*

*Daddy.*

As she agreed, a memory of one of those kinky videos popped into her brain, and she tried to shut down the spanking scene. She did not want him to sense that turned her on. Her anxiety skyrocketed, drawing her away from the magic of his lovemaking. He thrust inside her fully and stopped moving.

Khadar brushed her hair away from her face and spoke aloud for the first time since their connection had begun. "Shhh, Little One. There's nothing wrong with having fantasies. Just imagine what you would like me to do to you. Picture me in your mind. I do not wish to have another man in our bed."

"You're not turned off?"

"I'm balls deep in your tight pussy. Our bond is the closest I've ever heard of. Mate, we are perfectly matched. What you find stimulating, I do as well. I don't want to be anywhere else with anyone else. You are truly my mate."

She could read the truth in his gaze. *Move!*

Instantly, he withdrew and surged inside her. His attention wiped out her slight freak-out. Feeling closer to him than she'd dreamed possible, Lalani didn't worry about what he would see in her mind. She caught hints of his desires as well. Lalani deliberately pictured him taking her from behind and binding her completely to drive his arousal higher.

"Princess." He pushed the warning from between gritted teeth.

When she thought she couldn't come again, he pushed her into a fast climax that took her breath away. Khadar continued to power into her with several deep thrusts until he shouted his pleasure into the room. Draping over her as their bodies calmed, he pressed a hundred kisses to her face, neck, and shoulders.

His withdrawal made her ache for him even though her body couldn't take any more. He gathered her close to him and kissed her temple.

*Rest now, Mate.* He plucked Lettuce from his perch on the headboard and placed him in her arms.

She nestled against Khadar's side, letting him support her. Even the bright morning light couldn't keep her from submitting to her exhaustion.

# Chapter 5

When Khadar's mate woke, he watched her wince as she moved. Lalani would need some tender loving care.

"Good afternoon, Princess."

"Afternoon? Did I sleep that long?" She looked horrified. "I'm so sorry. You should have shoved me off."

Enchanted by her, Khadar treasured her sweet embarrassment. "That's never going to happen, Princess. The other dragons are aware that I will be scarce as our bond matures."

"Is that a fancy way to say as we screw?"

A laugh burst from his lips. "Making love is not the only part of connecting with one's mate, Lalani." He studied her face, trying to decide if she was embarrassed or if something else was going on. He wanted to know all of her thoughts but restrained himself from diving into her mind.

"So, they don't know we're having sex?"

*Oh, they know that.*

"Khadar!" Her exclamation confirmed the thought that everyone was aware they were physically involved flustered her. Well, more than involved. Their bond had blown him away as well. He'd never heard of the mates' brains being linked while the dragon was in human form—not without assistance.

"I understand, Princess. Everyone wishes us well and would never judge you."

"Not the Petersons."

"Wipe them from your mind, Lalani. They will not bother you again. Now, I am going to run a hot bath for you to soak away any tenderness. Then we'll get something to eat before I show you around your new home."

"Oh, I'd like that. Can you get hot water?"

"Dragons are collectors. The nonelectric water heating system from years ago is in working order." He sat up and lifted her onto his lap.

"That has to be a hundred years old." She marveled before remembering who she was talking to. "How old are you?"

"Not as ancient as the mountains but close. Set Lettuce on the pillow. He needs more sleep," Khadar instructed and paused for her to follow his directions.

When she did, he praised her, "Good girl." Rising from the bed with her cradled in his arms, Khadar walked toward the bathroom.

"You're kidding, right? You can't be just slightly younger than the mountains."

"No, Little One. I have watched over Wyvern since the beginning." He set her feet on the tile. "Go potty."

Turning on the water to fill the old-fashioned clawfoot tub while she used the toilet, he jumped into the separate, clear-walled shower. Cold water pelted down on him from the wide showerhead. She came back into the main area and stopped to stare at him. Just the feel of her eyes on his shaft made it react. As she approached, studying his body displayed under the cascade, she saw his shaft thicken and lift. Tempted, she opened the door. Warm air drifted in displaying the chill inside.

"Brrr!"

"Go check the water in the tub, Princess. It's too cold in here for you."

Pouting slightly, she let him close the door. He watched her walk the short distance to the tub before she turned back around to observe him shower. His body couldn't resist her allure. His cock had responded immediately to her interest.

The temptress rested one hand on the edge of the tub and leaned over to swirl the other through the water as if she were testing the temperature. The view of her bottom directed deliberately his way made him dunk his head under the cold water as he struggled for control. She was already sore. He squeezed the base of his cock hard as he drowned himself.

When he'd regained his composure, Khadar stepped back from the spray and looked for her. She sat on the edge of the tub, still focused on the shower. As he stared at her, resisting her allure with every fiber of his being, Lalani spread her legs and brushed a hand up her inner thigh. When she reached her pussy, he came out of the shower with a roar.

As he stalked forward, she widened her legs and rubbed her pink folds. He could see how wet she was already.

*Hands behind your back!*

She moved slowly as if debating whether or not to comply. He knew she'd decided the minute she smiled at him. Locking eyes with him, she traced her wet opening.

Striding toward his naughty mate, Khadar scooped her up with an arm around her waist. As she dangled over his forearm, he remembered to turn off the water before sitting down to drape Lalani over his lap. Admiring her sweet curves, he landed his first swat before she understood what he had planned.

"Nooooo!" she wailed as he smacked her vulnerable bottom several times in succession. "I don't want to get spanked, Khadar."

"Daddy," he corrected as he continued to spank her. He loved the feel of her smooth skin under his palm. Her skin took on a rosy hue. "What did I say?"

"Something I didn't choose to do. I suppose you're going to demand I look at you too," she answered petulantly, staring at him.

*Wrong answer.*

As her spanking continued, Khadar watched her face. He saw the exact moment her mind stopped telling her to fight and she submitted to his control. She drooped over his lap with tears dripping to the tile below her, and he rubbed her pink bottom.

"You don't let me have any fun," she accused him.

"You were doing an excellent job of seducing me, Princess. But you're already sore. Making love to you now would not be enjoyable for you."

"It might be."

He traced the cleft of her bottom to her drenched opening. Her body had enjoyed her spanking. Monitoring her expression, he slipped a finger into her pussy and stopped as she winced again. "My penis is much larger than my finger."

She nodded her agreement. Lalani looked down at the ground, unable to maintain eye contact as she whispered, "But I enjoyed our time together last night. I want to feel like that again."

"You will, Princess. I promise. But now, you need to let me take care of you." He lifted her from his thighs and sat her on his lap. Tilting her face up, Khadar kissed her tearstained cheeks.

"Now. Let's get you into the tub so Daddy can bathe you."

Khadar rose and lowered her gently into the water. Her hiss when the hot water touched her bottom made him hide a smile. She was absolutely adorable. He felt his cock twitch and sternly controlled his desire. She was not used to taking him and needed time to recover. Soaking would reduce the sting from her punished cheeks as well.

"Daddy?"

"Yes, Lalani."

"You're still..."

Her voice trailed off as he lowered himself to kneel next to the tub. He guessed, "Naked?"

She nodded and then added, "Hard."

Picking up a soft washcloth, he dipped it in the water before answering. "That's going to happen frequently around you, Princess."

"Do you need me to help you?"

"With my cock?" he asked, not sure what she was offering as he dispensed sweet-smelling soap on the damp cloth.

Another nod confirmed that guess, and he took her arm to wash. He spread lather over her skin before answering, "I will give you permission to touch or taste me another day, mate. Today is not good for you."

"Really?" When he inclined his head, she added, "But that's not fair to you."

"My cock will be fine if we stop talking about it."

She considered that for a few seconds then started giggling. "Sorry, Daddy."

"You are not. Lying to Daddy gets you spanked faster than not following my directions," he warned. "Close your eyes so I can wash your face."

"I'm not in trouble?" She tilted her chin up.

"No, Princess. You're adorable, and I can't believe how lucky I am to have you as my mate." He pressed a kiss to her lips before reining himself in and continuing her bath.

"I'm lucky too."

He rewarded that with a kiss against her palm as he washed her arm.

"What would have happened if I'd never come back to Wyvern?"

"I would not have had a mate until you passed away. Then the next possible mate would have to be born and mature," he explained.

"That could be years!"

"I hope you would have had a very long, happy life if we hadn't met," Khadar assured her.

"Even if that meant you were alone?"

"Yes, Princess. Whether you're my mate or not, your existence is important. I would never wish that to end. Toes next," he requested.

She lifted one leg out of the water to wiggle those digits at him. He cradled her heel in his hand and cleaned her foot, paying special attention to her sole. Lalani couldn't keep herself from giggling. Her reflective mood dissolved.

"Ticklish much?" he said with a grin.

"Not normally. I think you have the magic touch."

He winked and said, "Indeed."

Khadar washed her leg and softly smoothed over her pussy, washing her arousal away. He cupped her bottom with one hand and lifted her off the tub floor to whisk between her buttocks. She realized he was going to take care of her completely. Allowing her to settle back down on the porcelain, Khadar cleaned her other leg.

"Keep your legs spread. Let the warm water ease your soreness," he commanded as he moved onto her torso.

His soft and soothing touch shouldn't have aroused her... but this was Khadar touching her. She knew how he could make her feel. When he didn't use any of his super sexy Daddy moves, Lalani was disappointed.

"No pouting, Princess. I will enjoy your sweet curves completely at another time."

"I'm better now," she assured him.

"I'm glad."

Snorting at his obvious stubbornness, Lalani dropped one hand from the edge of the tub into the water. A plume of water spouted up and splashed over Khadar's powerful chest.

"I didn't mean to do that," Lalani assured him.

"Right," he answered skeptically.

"No, really. I'm sorry."

"Apology accepted, Lalani. Next time, I'll know it's not an accident."

"Yes, Daddy."

In a few minutes, he finished bathing her. Khadar rose smoothly to his feet. "Stay there until I come back to help you out. It will be a while before the water cools."

"Um, Daddy." His cock was impressive.

"I know, Princess. Being near you excites me."

As he walked away, she waited to feel pain as the mate bond stretched between them. There was some discomfort remaining when he moved away, but the pain of separation had eased.

*Princess. I am close.*

*You can still hear my thoughts?*

*Yes. Our connection is strong. If it bothers you, I can show you how to dampen it.*

How much of what was going on in her brain did she

want him to know? Was it healthy for him to be aware of what she was thinking? What if she got furious?

She waited for Khadar to comment on that concern, but he was quiet. He had decided many things for her. This seemed to be something she had control over. Lalani liked that Khadar trusted her either way. What man wanted to be alerted if their woman checked out another man?

Khadar appeared in the bathroom wearing jeans that hugged his thick thighs. As she devoured his appearance, Khadar walked toward her. She held up her hands for him to help her from the tub. Instead, he leaned over her to grip each side of her torso and lifted her effortlessly out of the water.

"You will not look at other dragons," he breathed. That telltale flash of green told her to tread lightly.

"Of course not, Daddy," she assured him as he wrapped a towel around her.

"Good girl."

# Chapter 6

*Khadar! We need you.*

He looked across the dining room table to his precious mate. Khadar had not expected an early morning crisis. Not that they occurred on a time schedule.

"Princess, we need to join the other dragons. There's a problem on the border."

"I get to go with you?" Lalani asked, looking nervous.

"Yes. The mate bond is still too rigid for that distance. It will stretch it to the point of pain once again until you adjust to it, allowing it to relax. Wrap up your toast in a napkin and meet me by the front door," he instructed, pointing from the dining room toward the correct path. Soon, she would be able to stay on his mountain without him. That could take days or months.

Thank goodness he'd prepared for this. Running into the bedroom, he opened a cabinet and grabbed a pair of headphones. Retracing his steps, he discovered the entryway was empty. Following the mate bond, Khadar located Lalani in the kitchen. She'd made a wrong turn.

"This house is like a maze. I'm never going to find my way around it," Lalani said, pink tinging her cheeks.

"You will. Give yourself a bit of grace. Soon you'll be romping around like you've lived here forever. Now, let us be off. Something urgent awaits."

"What are those for?" She pointed at the item he'd retrieved.

"To protect your ears." He ushered her outside.

"From what?" she asked, allowing herself to be rushed through the door.

"I can get noisy. I don't want your hearing damaged."

"Oh. Okay." She stood still as he adjusted them to fit comfortably on her head.

Moving away from the house, Khadar shifted rapidly. When Lalani had climbed into position and held on tightly to his scales, he launched himself into the air. Her awe and excitement at flying in the daylight made him remember how his first flight had blown his mind. He eavesdropped on her thoughts and appreciated seeing everything through her eyes.

The ancient town stretched below them, surrounded by rings of increasingly modern homes and businesses. Wyvern had changed much over the years. The majestic mountains shone in the morning light and reached into the clouds.

Suspecting she had forgotten, Khadar reminded his mate, *Finish your breakfast.*

*Okay. Your dragon is very pretty. Your scales glow like your eyes.*

*Thank you, Princess.*

Inside, his dragon felt like making happy loops. Controlling the distraction of his inner joy, Khadar focused on spotting the trouble that had forced the alert. There. Something or someone under the tree cover had disturbed bronze dragons.

*Khadar. Sorry to disturb you during your mating.* Oldrik turned in a large circle over a forested section.

If something had caught the attention of the eldest dragon in the horde, Khadar was automatically concerned.

*Oh, he's pretty. All blue like water but with sparkles.*

*Remember that part about not looking at other dragons?* Khadar reprimanded her.

*I'm checking out his scales.*

*Harrumph.*

Oldrik interrupted their exchange. *Khadar, there is a group of rebels who attacked the settlers at the gate after asking for entrance into Wyvern.*

Lalani stroked his neck to reassure him, and Khadar focused on Oldrik's update. The corridor leading to the gates controlled by the dragons was a safe zone. They only allowed people inside if they passed the screening and had some tie to Wyvern or a skill that was needed. The dragons' guards protected those in line while they waited.

*What happened?*

*They accosted those waiting to be granted permission to enter and robbed them of their belongings. When men following our guidelines banded against the thieves, the marauders took an unprotected family hostage.*

*So, there are innocents with the aggressors?*

*No.*

That word resonated in his head. Oldrik didn't have to tell him. The men had killed the family. What if one was a mate or would have become a mate? Anger filled his mind.

*Daddy? You're okay.* Lalani hugged his neck hard. The last bits of her toast tumbled to the ground. Khadar suspected she had lost them in her rush to comfort him.

*Thank you, Princess. I'm glad you're here. Make sure your headphones are directly over your ears. Press them tight.*

*Daddy?*

*It will be all right.*

Khadar noticed a movement under a section of the forested area. He listened for heartbeats hidden under the cover of the trees. One. Two. Three. Four. He pinpointed their locations and roared a warning to the wildlife. Birds exploded from the trees. Instinctively, they knew to flee from what would come.

Redirecting his attention, Khadar scanned the area for other dragons and found none. Oldrik had obviously warned the rest of the horde to vacate the area. Khadar checked to make sure Oldrik was far enough away and saw the last of the blue dragon's silhouette on the horizon.

*Make sure your headphones are on securely, Princess.*

*They're in place, Daddy.*

He opened his mouth and roared. A blast from a green dragon could be either fire or death. Khadar focused his lethal bellow on that forested patch. One. Two. Three. Where was the fourth? Zeroing in on his location, Khadar directed the sound toward the fleeing murderer. Four. The heartbeats below him were silent.

*It's done.*

Oldrik acknowledged his message first. The other dragons echoed the declaration.

Part of his mind had monitored Lalani's health during the retribution. The frequency of his specialized roar could interrupt the electric connections in the cells of animals, killing them almost instantly. He did not regret that the process was painful.

*You can take off your headphones, Lalani. Are you okay?*

Her arms loosened around his neck as she followed his direction. *I don't understand what happened.*

## Khadar

*I know, mate. Green dragons have a special power. That's why Oldrik called me.*

*The birds all flew away.*

*I warned the innocent creatures. Hopefully, they heeded my call.*

*There were those who were guilty of something?* Lalani swallowed hard, and Khadar could feel the swell of her emotions.

*Yes. There was an attack at the gate. A woman and her children were killed as they waited to be screened to enter Wyvern.*

*Why would someone do that?*

*The change, losing technology and all its tools, has brought out the worst in some. If I had to guess, they were after the scant supplies she'd lugged on their trek.*

After a pause, Lalani responded. *She was so close to being safe.*

Khadar could hear the pain in her voice as Lalani sympathized with those murdered. She had a tender heart. He wished he could protect her from everything but knew that was impossible.

*This will not be allowed to happen on our land. Dragon justice is swift.*

Lalani was quiet for several minutes as Khadar flew. He could hear her ragged breath and knew she grieved for those lost. He headed for a special place at the base of his mountain. Scanning the area for any intruders, Khadar landed in a meadow once he was sure there was no one around.

*We are alone, Princess.*

Lalani scrambled down. *Where are we?*

Shifting as soon as she was clear, Khadar strode toward his mate and gathered her in his arms.

"I thought a favorite spot of mine might distract you." He took her hand and led her down a path. Birds of all colors darted around the surrounding trees. Their music provided a cheerful chorus.

"I'm sorry you have to dole out judgement."

"I am too. In many ways, the crash of technology tore apart the civilization that existed before. With everyone focused on survival, there are no police officers, judges, or jails."

"What happened to those in jail?" she asked, as if thinking through this for the first time. "They couldn't still be trapped after all these weeks."

"Most were automatically released from their cells."

Many convicts would focus only on reaching their families, but the most hardened criminals would see the state of society as a free-for-all. The dragons had protected Wyvern for centuries. This level of lawlessness, however, hadn't occurred for many years.

"Come, Princess. You must see this." He led the way around a thicket of berries and held the branches armed with thorns out of the way for her to pass without being scratched.

He watched her face as she stepped onto the bank of a small spring and loved the expression of awe that illuminated her features. The water emerged from the ground above and cascaded into a watering hole. Lalani's gaze darted everywhere, taking in the sparkling waterfall and the abundance of flowers.

"Wow! This is gorgeous."

"Would you like to go for a swim?"

"I didn't bring a suit."

"Neither did I," he reassured her and yanked his shirt over his head.

An impish glint shone from her eyes, and Lalani pulled

off the tunic she wore and tossed it onto a rock. As she worked on stripping off her leggings, Khadar stepped out of his shoes and removed the rest of his clothes. Kneeling at her feet, Khadar settled Lalani on one bent knee as he got rid of her shoes and the tangle of stretchy material from her legs.

When she was nude, he scooped her into his arms and rose to his feet. Striding into the pool, he watched her reaction to the chilly water. Her nipples tightened the minute her bottom touched the surface.

"It's freezing!" she shrieked.

"There's only one way to get used to it. Hold your breath," he ordered. He turned around and fell backward into the deeper water.

"You!" she sputtered when she surfaced to tread water as she pushed her hair from her face.

"Me. I did it. How does the water feel now?"

Khadar reached out to pull her close to the warmth of his body. She wrapped her arms and legs around his torso, plastering herself against him. The feel of her wet curves was irresistible. He leaned down to kiss her lips.

Several sizzling kisses later, he asked that same question again. "Any warmer?"

She wiggled around a bit, swishing the water with one arm. "I'm good. It's refreshing. Did you do your dragon heat thing?"

"No, Princess. I would not disturb the creatures that frequent this watering spot."

Instantly, she plastered herself against him, trying to climb out of the water. "Creatures? What creatures?"

"You're always safe with me, Lalani. Look into the water. See the minnows? They nibble all the moss off the rocks, keeping the water clean."

"Oh, those are okay." She relaxed a bit before pointing. "Look! That's a big fish."

"Those big fish keep the minnows from filling the pool. There are turtles and other creatures in and around the water."

"Snakes?"

"No snakes allowed."

"Really?" she questioned, glancing in all directions. "There's like a snake fence?"

Laughter rumbled deep in his chest as he tried to keep a straight face. She must have heard the noise because she turned back to look at him.

"You!" she rebuked him. Smacking his chest, she joined his merriment. Her giggles enchanted him. "That had to be the stupidest question ever."

"Not stupid, Lalani. You're just not used to predators. I like to bathe here in dragon form as well. Most creatures will avoid contact with more powerful predators."

"Do you eat snakes?"

This time he couldn't control his guffaw at the disgust on her face. He pulled her close to kiss that expression away. When he lifted his lips from hers, Khadar shook his head.

"You don't?"

"I could if I were desperate. But you could do that in human form too."

"No, I couldn't." She looked completely appalled by that idea.

"You wouldn't want to, but you could. Snake bites, snake fricassee, snake soup…"

"No, no, and definitely no," she answered. A second later, Lalani asked, "What's fricassee?"

This time, she joined in his joyous laughter. His mate was the most precious thing on earth. Tightening his arms around her, Khadar reveled in the delight she'd brought to his life. She became more essential to his life with each passing day.

"You delight me, Little One."

"I heard Ciel call Argenis 'Daddy.' Are all dragons Daddies?"

"I cannot answer for all of my breed, Princess. Dragons are definitely dominant creatures at the top of the food chain."

"Alpha males, hmmm?"

"Yes."

Lalani looked at their surroundings and relaxed against him. Waves of contentment came from her. His answers must've satisfied the questions she'd pondered upon for a while. He didn't add more, nor did he dive into her mind.

"Are you happy with our mental connection, Lalani? Do you want me to show you how to shield your thoughts from me?"

"Am I bothering you?" she asked, studying his face once again.

"Never."

"I'm happy. It makes me feel safer to know I can think at you," she confessed.

Shielding the anger that gathered inside him, Khadar cursed the Petersons for bringing peril to her life. "Then we won't change anything. I enjoy being connected to you as well."

Khadar shifted them, moving to float on his back with Lalani balanced on top of him. She squirmed a bit before finding a comfortable spot.

"You're hard," she explained.

"Always when I'm with you." He knew she could feel his erection against her, just as he could smell her arousal.

"We could..."

"Let your body recover." He finished her proposition.

"You are Mr. No Fun."

"That's Daddy No Fun to you," he corrected before wrapping his arms around her and sinking under the water to dunk them both.

The resulting water battle was epic.

# Chapter 7

Later that afternoon when they returned for lunch, Lalani surprised herself by automatically climbing onto Khadar's lap. She felt better close to him and could sense how much he enjoyed holding her in his arms. She looked around the beautiful dining room, appreciating the lovely décor. It was elegant but not stuffy.

"Here, Princess. Try this." Khadar picked up a slice of yellow cheese from the charcuterie board in front of them. There was also an assortment of fresh fruit and vegetables.

"That cheese tastes amazing. It's so fresh," she said, taking another bite.

"Ciel helps make this on Argenis's mountain."

"Really? I don't do anything. I need to contribute somehow."

"Being my mate is a big adjustment. Give yourself some time. Perhaps you'll find something you like to try. The wine grapes are almost ripe. How do you feel about stomping grapes?"

"Like with my feet?"

"The old manual presses work, but sometimes it's best to do things by hand or, in this case, by feet."

"I would love to try that." She paused for a moment before suggesting, "Could we ask Ciel and Aurora? Maybe they would have fun too?"

"That is an excellent idea. We can make a day of it." Khadar agreed. "We'll have to wait until the harvest, of course. That will be several months away."

"Are those the only dragon mates? I don't want anyone to be left out," Lalani said. "How many dragons are there?"

"In our horde, there are nine dragons. Four have mates now."

"So, there is one mate other than Aurora, Ciel, and me?" Lalani asked.

"Yes. The Amethyst dragon's mate, Yolanda. She is older and prefers to stay in Tyrian's home. Throughout our history, the horde has worked together, but each dragon is... well, secretive."

"I can understand that. You know, hoarders and all," she teased.

"Keepers of treasurers. We are united as a horde but still solitary in our pursuit of gathering riches. Mates are a prize as well. In the past, mates never socialized."

Lalani struggled to not project how she'd feel without friends and judge that lifestyle. She knew some people didn't need social interaction. That definitely wasn't her.

"So, Yolanda has been secluded for years. I can understand that she's comfortable with her mate. It makes sense that she's adapted well and has people that live on the Amethyst dragon's mountain to talk to. I'm glad I've met Ciel and Aurora. They were nice to me."

"That is why I'm allowing you to interact with them."

Lalani bristled at that idea. She wasn't used to someone permitting her to do anything.

"Eat, Princess," he said, gently holding a bite to her lips.

Automatically, she opened her mouth. As she chewed, Lalani's ire dissipated. Khadar would care for her as he thought best. She could rail against his control, or she could enjoy it. Looking down at his huge hand spanning her thigh, Lalani admitted to herself that being a dragon's mate was more than she'd ever imagined possible.

"After lunch, you'll take a nap in your nursery."

"I don't need a nap."

Khadar didn't argue. He just fed her another bite.

Did he say a nap in her nursery? Lalani remembered all those books she'd read. That special room usually held toys and provided a space Littles could claim as their own.

"I have a nursery?" she asked excitedly.

"Yes, Lalani. I guessed what my mate would like. If you don't like the decorations or the color, tell me, and I'll change it."

Torn between not wanting to nap and the desire to see whatever he was calling a nursery, Lalani's thoughts whirled in her mind as she sat eating whenever he held something to her lips.

"You are so quiet, Princess. Are you unwell?"

"No. I feel okay." She waited a fraction of a second before adding, "Can I go see the nursery?"

"Of course. If you're hungry after your nap, you may have a snack."

She nodded eagerly and scrambled off his lap. Taking his hand after he stood, Lalani followed him down the hallway toward their bedroom. Confused, she glanced up at him.

"It's a private space, Princess, and a protected one. Come through the closet."

Never having walked into the closet, Lalani looked at the immense space with clothing and shoes. She noticed a few pretty dresses hanging up on one side. Dropping her Daddy's hand, she raced forward to check them out.

"Whose are these?"

"Those are for you. Do you want to change into one after your nap?" he asked.

She nodded before she realized she'd just agreed to a nap. Her jaw stretched open in a wide yawn. Maybe sleep was just what she needed. Not that she planned on telling Khadar.

"Open that door, Lalani. That leads into the nursery."

After twisting the knob and pushing it into the room, she stepped into an area unlike anything she'd ever seen. "What? This is amazing." She gasped as she turned in a circle in the center of the room. "It looks just like the watering hole from this morning."

The carpet was blue, and the walls were all painted as if they were the banks. "Look! There's the berry bush we went around. And there's that wacky-looking tree with the low branches that hang over the water."

She pointed, tracing one branch as it extended over the ceiling. "And all the birds!

"There's Lettuce!" Lalani ran forward to scoop up the green dragon stuffie. "How did he get in here?"

"Dragons can be full of tricks."

She hugged Lettuce to her chest before showing him around the room. Lalani knew Khadar must have placed him in the crib while she was distracted, but it was fun to imagine him exploring on his own.

"I guess you like the décor?" he asked when she returned to his side. "Look around the room. There are fun things gathered there in the toy chest. Games. Puzzles. Books."

She could hear the happiness in his voice. A thought jumped into her head. Lalani blurted it out. "Did you make this room for your last mate?"

He looked like she had hit him. Lalani felt bad immediately. She'd never seen him appear anything other than dragon strong.

"No, Princess. When my last mate was part of my life, that area of my mountain didn't exist. Two years ago, we dug for a new well and tapped the underground spring. It formed the waterfall and gradually created the watering hole. I decorated this to share my favorite spot with my new mate whenever I would be lucky enough to find her."

"I'm sorry. I shouldn't have even thought that."

"It is better to ask than to worry. Even as connected as we are, I wouldn't have realized something was bothering you unless you thought hard about it. Then I wouldn't have known what troubled you," he told her. "I want you to promise to tell me if you're concerned."

She walked to him instead of the play area he indicated and wrapped her arms around his waist. "I'm sorry. You were so happy to show this to me, and I spoiled it."

"If you enjoy your nursery, then you haven't ruined anything," he told her. "Come sit on my lap and ask me questions."

He led her to an oversized rocking chair and helped her up on his thighs. "What would you like to know?"

"How many mates have you had?"

"Six. They were in all shapes and sizes. I love each one and remember our time together happily."

Lalani thought about it. She was torn. It was hard to know he had cared about others. But she also wouldn't have wanted him to be alone for years. A thought popped into her mind. "You say love in the present tense. Do you still love them?"

"Of course. It is not the passionate, in-person love like I have for you but a fond love for the years I was lucky to have them in my life."

"You love me?" Lalani asked, studying his face. Her heart beat faster. She couldn't believe how much she cared for Khadar so quickly.

"From the moment I saw you," he said simply.

"Just because of the mate bond?"

"In the beginning, yes. Now, no. I love your quick mind, your arousing body, your tender heart, and everything that makes you... you."

"I feel for you more than anyone I've ever met. Is that love?" she asked.

"I hope it is or will be in the future. We have not been together long, Princess. Feelings grow deeper with time."

She rested her head against his broad chest and allowed him to rock her. Listening to his heavy heartbeat, Lalani looked around the room he'd created for her. It was his favorite place on his mountain, and he'd chosen to share it with her. That meant something.

"This room is so pretty. I love it."

"I'm glad, Lalani. Everyone needs a space to call their own. I hope this will be your special place. You've had so many stressful things happen to you. Finding your birth mother, losing her, the change, the mate bond..."

"It's been crazy. She had to give me up. My birth mom that is. My dad's family was from Hawaii, and he was so handsome. He was gone when she found out. His grandmother, Lalani, was ill. The family returned to Hawaii to care for her. My birth mother was only fifteen and knew she couldn't take care of me. She made the placement agency let her name me and choose who adopted me."

"Did she select well?" Khadar asked. She could hear the concern in his voice and lifted her head to look at him.

"She did. They were the best. I miss them too."

"Of course you do. I'm sorry your life has included such sorrow, Lalani."

"And happiness. She was overjoyed when I contacted her and invited me immediately to come visit. I put it off for a little bit, thinking it would be weird. It wasn't. I'm sorry I wasted days I could have spent with her."

Khadar's fingers smoothed away tears she didn't even know she was crying. "I'm glad you got to talk to her, Lalani."

"Me too."

Lalani laid her head back on Khadar's chest and finally let herself sob. Her birth mother had been a stranger, but Lalani would never forget the short time they'd had together. He held her, rocking her slightly from side to side as she mourned her loss. His lips pressed a kiss to her hair, and she tilted her mouth up to meet his. His lips touched hers softly to reassure her.

When he lifted his head, she whispered, "I've only felt truly comfortable around four people in my life. My parents. My birth mother. And..."

"And who, Princess?"

She swallowed hard and forced herself to tell him the truth. "And you."

His fingers stroked through her hair. "That makes me very happy, Lalani."

"It makes me happy too. You make me happy."

His next kiss went straight to her heart. He loved her. There was no way she could mistake the level of his feelings.

She poured her emotions into her response and felt his heart skip a beat under her hand. She didn't need to say the words yet. He understood.

# Chapter 8

Watching Lalani sleep in the narrow bed in her nursery had become one of Khadar's favorite activities. After that first nap left her refreshed and unstressed, he'd put her down each afternoon. She always fussed. Yesterday, she'd had a very red bottom by the time he convinced her to stay in bed when he placed her there. Today, she'd climbed under the covers herself and waited to be tucked in.

*Khadar?*

*Is something wrong, Ardon?*

The bronze dragon was a loner—even more reclusive than the other dragons in the horde. Well, excluding Keres. Fighting the darkness that came from missing a mate for so long made the black dragon shun interactions. The bronze dragon, however, was still a mystery even after so many years.

*There are signs of trespassers navigating between Oldrik's mountain and mine. I have notified him as well.* Ardon's voice was tense.

*Is there a road or a pass there?*

*Not for a hundred years. I am following the trail. They are strategically staying under the cover of the forest.*

*I'm coming.* Ardon's report concerned him. While it could be innocent refugees, the vast majority would follow the protocol to gain admission.

After one last look at his sleeping mate, Khadar forced himself to stand and walk quietly from the room. He stopped at a blackboard pinned next to the door and wrote in green chalk: *Dragon business. I'll be back.*

Once in flight, he headed for the bronze's and blue dragon's mountains, spotting the two immediately as they circled over an isolated thatch of trees. As he drew near, Khadar roared. Immediately, the other dragons answered. That sound should terrify whoever was below.

Plumes of colored smoke curled into the sky, obstructing their view. It was as if a thousand smoke bombs from the old fireworks stands had been detonated. Blue, red, and green pillars rose into the sky. Khadar wheeled off to avoid breathing in the chemicals. Something smelled wrong.

*Danger! Beware the fumes!* Khadar warned.

*Too late. Dizzy.*

Khadar wheeled, heading back toward Oldrik. He had to try to help, even if he put himself in danger. Sending a burst of flame toward the colored smoke, he hoped the fire would eliminate any possible peril. A weird musical tune distracted him for a second, and he shook his head to clear his thoughts.

Refocusing, he continued on his path. The crash of a huge collision made Khadar wheel to the side. What had just happened in the smoky haze? Oldrik's gigantic form emerged from the thick colored mess, flying sideways as if from the impact. Ardon appeared after him, propelled by his own power. Khadar guessed Ardon had slammed into Oldrik, pushing him out of danger.

*Good job, Ardon!*

Khadar commended the bronze dragon as he watched

Oldrik settle in a safe place. Oldrik shook his snout, obviously trying to free his mind of whatever was in that smoke.

*I owe you one, Ardon. If I'd been inside any longer...* Oldrik's message faded.

*I'll collect someday, Oldrik.* Ardon brushed away his thanks. *For now, let's eliminate whoever is causing this. Can you use your sound, Khadar?*

*Wait! There are twelve people on the ground. Eleven are huddled together and appear to be shackled,* Oldrik reported.

At that report from Ardon, Khadar abandoned the idea of unleashing his special power.

*Ardon, would you like to join me on the ground to do some hunting?*

*Good idea.*

*Oldrik? What's your viability?*

*I'm eighty percent but improving. I'm with you.*

*I'll land in the north. Oldrik, take your side. Ardon, can you attack from the west?*

An affirmative roar from the bronze dragon triggered the release of more colored smoke into the air. *Gotcha!* The thick cover would keep the man orchestrating the attack from the ground from seeing the dragons had landed and shifted. Khadar sent a warning to Oldrik and Ardon.

*Watch for sensors hidden in the trees.*

Landing as softly as he could, Khadar shifted and moved with both care and urgency toward the small murmur of voices. In a few minutes, he could spot a man holding a long torch in his hand who focused on the obscured sky above.

Khadar glanced up. Immediately, he relayed the details.

*Above his head are bags tied to the trees. He is using a torch to reach and ignite them.*

*I'm here. I see them.*

With Ardon in place, Khadar moved closer. Pulling out a

knife, he prepared to eliminate the man wielding the torch. A flash to the left warned him, and Khadar dropped to the ground. A bolt glanced over his shoulders.

*Booby traps in the trees. I'm taking this guy out.*

Finding the widest spot between the trees, Khadar shifted. He would be the most vulnerable in the few seconds it took to change from man to beast. His armored sides snapped off a few trunks, toppling them to the forest floor. As soon as his transformation into dragon form finished, he roared a pinpointed line of fire over the heads of those shackled. The torchbearer erupted in flames and died within a fraction of a second. His attempt to ignite another bag failed due to the intensity of Khadar's attack.

"Well, that didn't last long." Ardon's voice carried from the other side of the camp. "I'll free these people."

"Hold off on that for a few," Oldrik suggested as he approached from the opposite direction.

"Thank you!" a woman called from the captives. "We didn't know how to warn you. They grabbed us from our camp and made us carry those bags up there."

Khadar didn't buy it. The victims could have easily overpowered one man. *This makes no sense.*

*Agreed.* Ardon moved closer to those secured together as if he were coming to free them. *Weapons under their cloaks. They're holding something in their fists.*

Seeing them move to raise their hands, Khadar opened his jaw and released his special call. The group dropped to the ground. Two additional thumps resounded sickeningly. The corpses all held weapons and small amounts of the toxic dust. The dragon shifters, even in human form, had weathered Khadar's roar without ill effects.

Khadar shifted and ran forward to investigate those other two figures. Bearing crossbows and bolts in quivers on their backs, the men had decorated themselves with leaves and twigs. Disguised from view, the tree had provided cover, but the sound had terminated them in a split second.

"What is going on?" Khadar wondered aloud.

"The organization of this attack is concerning. It was deliberate in the attempt to injure dragons with whatever was in that smoke. And to shackle people together to make it look like a kidnapping?" Oldrik shook his head in disbelief.

"I agree, Oldrik. Whoever devised this endeavor to lure us in is trying to eliminate dragons," Ardon stated. His face was chiseled in anger.

"We need to find out what's in that smoke. And, even more important, who knew that it would affect dragons? Oldrik, what did it do to you?" Khadar asked.

"I inhaled on the way into the cloud and got some of that in my snout. Instantly, I was disoriented, like I couldn't tell which way was up and down. Landing was a problem. In my mind, I was soaring upward," Oldrik explained. "I concentrated on one tree and used that to guide my descent. Thank you, Ardon. I can't imagine what effect prolonged exposure would have had."

"I saw you rotate. It was obvious something was wrong," Ardon said.

"Our first priority is to determine the substances in that smoke," Khadar stated firmly.

"There is a chemist in town. He's concentrated on emergency medicines, but I'm sure he'd run some tests for us," Oldrik said.

"Let's do it. Look around for something we can use to transport a sample. Then we'll burn this from a distance," Khadar suggested.

Within a short time, Oldrik created long tongs from branches and vines. He maneuvered two of the small bundles from the disguised "victims" and placed them in a nested set of plastic containers holding food for the attackers.

"I'll carry it back to Wyvern," Oldrik volunteered. "I can find the chemist."

"Let's do this as quietly as possible," Ardon said.

"The horde needs to be alerted," Khadar decreed.

"Definitely. Humans on a need-to-know basis," Oldrik agreed.

After scouting the surrounding area for any additional chemical bags, Khadar and Ardon cleared the brush around to create a firebreak. Khadar was glad he wasn't alone to tromp through the woods in dragon form, knocking down all the vegetation like a dragon-shifter demolition.

*Be a dragon, they said. Live a glamorous life.*

Khadar couldn't keep from snorting at Ardon's joke. Just a few more yards and they'd have enough done to torch the area before returning home.

After that close call, he needed to hold Lalani.

# Chapter 9

*Dragon business?*

Rolling her eyes as she yawned, Lalani stretched, trying to wake up completely. She hated to admit it, but she felt better after the nap he made her take. Her clothes had disappeared from her dresser where he usually put them. She'd have to pick out something new.

Pushing back the covers, she then walked to the closet with her arms wrapped around herself. According to Khadar, she slept better naked. There was no arguing with him. He'd just pull the Daddy card—*Daddy makes the decisions.*

It was tough choosing a new outfit. Already, she had gotten spoiled by Khadar deciding everything for her. It was so much easier to enjoy the fun things without having to worry about all those adult responsibilities. Bills, cooking, laundry, cleaning... Those were definitely not on Lalani's favorite activity list.

Khadar had created a list of chores for her. They were on a big board in her nursery. Each day, she got a check mark or an X. Lots of check marks earned her a reward. Her face heated at the special rewards she had received. Too many Xs and she either had to stand in the corner or receive some other punishment.

Her eyes darted to the silvery butt plug that sat on the dresser with a tube of lubricant. Khadar had declared her bottom training would begin tonight. She couldn't imagine that going into her. Maybe he was kidding?

Pushing her hand down into the front of her leggings, Lalani tried to convince herself that the thought of him pushing that device into her bottom did not turn her on. The slickness her fingers discovered proved she was. Lalani stroked through her pink folds. Tingles of pleasure gathered as she caressed herself.

Could he tell if she...? Lalani debated if she could lie back on the pillows of her nursery bed to make herself climax. Maybe just a quick one?

She shook her head. He'd pick up some clue.

She pulled her hand from her pants and wiped her juices onto her leggings before running over to the bed to make it and tuck Lettuce in. She needed to earn a reward tonight. Her body craved Khadar's masterful touch.

A shiver of evil slid down her spine, pushing her desires away. Something was wrong. Malevolence seemed to hover around Khadar. Was he okay?

Scared to distract him, Lalani locked down her ability to think something to Khadar with fierce determination. He needed to focus on whatever was happening. Singing the most frivolous songs in her head, she attempted to keep her mind busy as she tidied her nursery, restowing the toys she'd played with before her nap.

When she needed to get out of that room, Lalani wandered through the house, trying to map it out in her head. She avoided looking out the windows when she saw smoke bellowing upward. About the third time through by herself, she was getting the hang of navigating through the large rooms and allowed herself to celebrate.

*I'm proud of you, Princess.* His voice was tinged with pride.

*Khadar? Are you here?*

*I just landed outside.*

Lalani dashed through the hallway and out the front door. Khadar stood tall and strong. He didn't appear injured. She ran to throw herself up into his arms. Khadar caught her with ease. Plastered against him, Lalani held on tightly.

"Mate? Are you okay?" His hands stroked over her body as he alternated which one supported her.

"You're the one who was in danger. What happened? Are you hurt? I sang to keep smothering the worried messages out of my brain."

"Princess, you are the most important person in my life..."

Lalani interrupted him. "I don't want you to get hurt because I'm panicking. That feeling was so scary." She bit the side of her lips and winced slightly. She'd done that a lot while she tried to concentrate on a song.

"I'm so sorry. Let's figure out how to make things better."

Khadar kissed her forehead and carried her up the stairs to a cushioned seat in a secluded corner of the large porch. Holding her on his lap, he cupped her face. "Remember, dragon. I'm difficult to hurt."

"You were in peril today. I don't care how you try to sugarcoat it. There was something bad out there. Tell me what it was."

"We were investigating an invading force between Oldrik's and Ardon's mountains. There is no pass there, so they haven't set up barricades. Ardon will correct that now."

"Only Ardon? Is Oldrik hurt?"

"He's fine. There was a slight problem today, and Oldrik got the worst of it. He recovered quickly."

She studied his face. "You're not telling me the whole truth."

"A group attacked us today. That targeted attempt was a new complication that we hadn't dealt with before. We were a bit surprised but took care of the problem."

"I saw the plumes of smoke."

"The colored ones didn't go up too far." Khadar brushed her hair away from her face and tucked it behind her ear. He didn't meet her gaze.

Lalani put her hands on each side of his sculpted jaw and demanded, "Look at me. I didn't see those. Just the black. What was the colored smoke for?"

"I'm trying not to upset you, Lalani. Let me tell you what happened."

"Please!"

"A group set off a number of colored streams of smoke. I could tell from the smell it was evil and avoided running into it."

"Oldrik got hit?" she guessed. She'd known something was wrong. Lalani felt bad that she was relieved Oldrik had gotten the brunt of the attack instead of Khadar.

"He inhaled a small amount before Ardon knocked him into clean air."

"Ardon wasn't hurt?"

"No. And Oldrik is fine now."

"But he wasn't then," Lalani stated.

"He was off-balance but recovered."

"Did they affect anyone from Wyvern?" she asked, biting a spot on her lip again.

"Princess. You have to stop chewing on your lip. You've wounded yourself."

"I only do that when I'm worried."

"No citizen of Wyvern was injured."

She released his face to run her hands over his body. "You're sure the smoke didn't get you?"

"I'm fine, Lalani."

"That awful feeling was so scary. I felt that you were in danger."

"Do we need to tamp down our mental connection? That way frightening things won't bombard you?"

Lalani shook her head violently. "No. I want to know. Can you just teach me how to keep from bothering you?" she asked. "That's what I'm afraid of doing."

"Singing was smart. Anything that makes your brain work. Exercise, read, do a puzzle in your nursery."

She nodded. "I can do that, Daddy." Lalani rested her head on his shoulder. "I'm glad you're unharmed."

"Dragon."

"Right. You're a big, tough, indestructible dragon."

"I've set the table for you," Louise, the housekeeper, announced from the doorway.

"Come on, Princess. We'll both feel better after eating."

Lalani stayed close to her Daddy. Just being near him helped her relax. Sitting on his lap, she munched on a sandwich Khadar had created for her from all the delectable ingredients on the table. Somehow the ones he made were always more delicious than those she put together.

She froze when she heard Khadar humming one of the songs she'd sung while he was gone. "You could hear me. Thank goodness I didn't..." Lalani clamped her teeth together to keep from finishing that sentence.

"Didn't what, Princess? Were you thinking of doing something naughty?"

Lalani shook her head. "No, I ran around the house trying to memorize where everything was."

To distract him, she picked up a carrot stick from their communal plate and held it to his mouth. He took a bite with flaring nostrils.

"Are the carrots stinky?" she asked, lifting the other half to her nose. It smelled like a carrot. Lalani popped it into her mouth and chewed. Tasted like a carrot.

Khadar grabbed her hand and lifted it. He sniffed her fingers. "Is there something you want to tell me, Princess?"

"No? I forgot to wash my hands before dinner?" she guessed.

"No, Lalani. Did you touch yourself while I was gone?"

"Oh! Just when I went to the bathroom," she lied.

"So, when I take down your pants, I'm not going to find you slick and aroused?"

"Well, now you will. You're talking about it. My body is reacting." *He knows. Quick. Think of something to distract him. Why is my mind completely blank?*

"Let's see."

Grasping her waist, he lifted Lalani into the air to press his nose against her mound. "You are definitely turned on, Princess. But wait."

He turned her slightly to press his nose to her thigh. "I can smell your juices here, Lalani. On the same side as the hand you caressed yourself with. Want to change your story?"

She shook her head.

"Hmmm. It's too bad baby monitors don't work anymore. I could simply watch the replay."

Khadar sat her back on his lap and helped himself to a large portion of potato salad. "This is my favorite. Would you like to try it?" he asked, holding a bite to her lips.

Lalani accepted the bite and chewed as she watched his face. Was that it? He was going to accept her word for it. Her stomach twisted into knots as she kept her face composed.

When Khadar didn't bring it up but chatted about things going on in Wyvern, Lalani relaxed. She'd gotten away with it.

"I cleaned my toys up and made my bed when I woke up," she announced proudly.

"What a wonderful Little you are, Princess. We will go up to the nursery after dinner and count all your points. Do you think you'll earn a reward today?"

"Yes, Daddy. I will."

He nodded and offered her another bite of yumminess. When her stomach was full, she leaned against his broad chest. She'd never get used to how much food Khadar ate. She couldn't see an ounce of extra weight on him. His dragon form must require a ton of calories to keep him functioning. Lalani figured he raised livestock for a reason. A dragon needed a steady supply of nourishment.

Dismissing that from her mind, Lalani wondered what her reward would be. Khadar promised she would enjoy being good and regret poor decisions. Maybe it was chocolate. She hadn't had that for days.

## Chapter 10

By the time they finished dinner, she'd forgotten about getting caught. She slipped her hand into Khadar's as they walked to the nursery. Skipping with happiness as he concentrated completely on her, Lalani realized she'd never been a man's complete focus before. She hadn't gone out much, but phones, messages, and other people had always distracted her date. Khadar was one hundred percent engaged with her. She liked it a lot.

"Look what a great job you did in here. I am very impressed, Princess. Let's look at your board. You get a check for putting away your toys and one for making your bed after your nap."

He marked those off and hesitated. "Unfortunately, lying to your Daddy removes all the check marks and replaces them with Xs." He set down the green marker and picked up the black one. He crossed out the two at the bottom as well as the earlier ones that she'd earned.

"But I got up without complaining this morning, Daddy. And I drank every drop of my morning water!"

"Lies. Erase everything."

He referred back to the chart and counted up the negative marks. "You've earned a severe punishment today, Princess. Do you have anything you want to tell me?"

"Okay. I rubbed my fingers through my... private area before wiping my fingers on my thigh. But I didn't do it for long. I didn't make myself come. The rule is my pleasure belongs to you. I stopped."

"Thank you for telling me the truth, Lalani. I bet that makes you feel better," he said as he stripped her shirt off.

"Wait. I don't still get punished, right? I admitted what I'd did."

"Oh, yes. Confessing to a lie helps me trust you've learned your lesson. It doesn't wipe away your naughtiness," Khadar explained as he knelt on one knee in front of her to slip off her shoes and leggings. "Dragons have certain abilities."

"Like your sound blast?" She looked toward the headphones that hung on a hook by the door.

"Exactly. That's a green dragon's special power. Other colors have unique talents. All dragons, however, have one skill they share."

"Shifting?"

"Yes, but more than that. We all can tell when someone is lying. We can smell it."

"All lies?" Lalani's heart sank, and she swallowed hard.

"Every single one. Small and big."

"So, you can tell I wasn't making it up when I told you I stopped and didn't... Well, I didn't make myself come."

"Yes. I know that's the truth, Princess. Thank you for making the right decision."

"Oh, good. So, my punishment won't be too bad, right?"

"That is an incorrect assumption."

Khadar walked into the closet. Lalani followed him,

curious about what he was doing. She watched him press on the wall, causing a large section to rotate out. Peering around his bulk, she spotted a large supply area filled with different items. Khadar ignored them all to pull out a chair.

"Why's that in the wall, Daddy?"

"Because it's a special chair that is only used in very serious situations."

She swallowed hard. "I'm truly sorry for lying, and I'll never do it again."

"Yes, you will. And this chair will come out then as well. Scoot on back into your nursery. Let's get your punishment underway."

*Underway?* Was it going to last a long time?

Edging out of the way, Lalani shifted for Khadar to carry the folded chair into the nursery. She stood off to the side to watch as he set it up. It seemed to move funny. The center appeared to rotate. Was a chair supposed to adjust like that?

"Come here, Princess."

She dragged her feet, stepping as slowly as possible. Khadar didn't rush her, just waited patiently for her to join him.

"Daddy, it's too early to get ready for bed."

"It will be a bit until you go to sleep, Princess. Come sit on this chair."

"What are you going to do to me?" she asked as he lifted her up by circling her waist with his hand.

He didn't answer until he'd set her carefully on the chair and wrapped a thick band around her torso. Her breasts were bound under the thick material. Lalani wiggled slightly and felt the webbed material rub over her nipples slightly. "Put your hands on the armrests, please."

"I don't like this chair, Daddy."

"It will be a love/hate relationship, I'm afraid. Armrests," he reminded her.

Slowly, she shifted her hands to lie on the supports. Lalani watched him tether her forearms to the chair. Being held in place sent shivers of arousal through her. There was nothing she could do. He was in control. "I don't understand, Daddy. Why am I tied to the chair?"

"Little ones who touch themselves without permission lose that privilege. Now, I'm going to tilt you a bit. Don't worry. I'm right here," Khadar reassured her as he did something on the side and her chair shifted backward until her weight rested on her spine. Her hips were slightly elevated above her head, tilting her surroundings to a strange angle.

"That's perfect." He messed with the seat, and suddenly an entire section of it detached from the main support of the chair. "There we go."

Air passed over her most intimate areas, and she quickly squeezed her thighs and calves together to shield her now-exposed pussy.

"Thank you for reminding me, Lalani." He shifted her legs apart. Khadar was securing the first limb when she slid the other next to it and crossed her ankles out in midair.

"Being naughty with all those black marks today would not be recommended," Khadar warned in a tone that brooked no rebellion.

"I'm scared, Daddy," she whispered.

"I am not going to hurt you, Lalani. I couldn't do that. Are you going to be uncomfortable? Yes. In pain, no. Unless I have to spank you first for being uncooperative."

She studied his face, thoughts racing through her mind. Khadar couldn't be mean to her. Maybe this was better than a spanking? Shivering, she felt so exposed. Lalani tried not to respond to his dominance, but her body wasn't listening. He'd know she was turned on by how wet she was.

"I don't want a spanking," she whispered again.

"That's my good girl. Let's get you into position then, and you'll avoid that punishment."

While she considered his words, noting he called this punishment, Khadar easily restrained her calves against the front legs of the chair. He stepped back and looked at her body from a few feet away.

"Good girl."

Lalani blinked up at him. His praise meant everything to her.

He walked over to the dresser and picked up two items. Bringing them back to where Lalani was secured, he set the plug on her tummy as he slowly screwed off the top of the tube of lubricant.

"Daddy, no." She shook her head frantically. It was heavy and cold against the small area where it touched her skin unlike the thick binding around her torso.

"Yes, Princess. Relax for me. That will make this easier on you." He spread the slippery gel around her small entrance he'd exposed in her position. "Deep breath. Hold it. Now exhale." His finger slid through that tight ring of muscles and into her bottom.

Nothing was off limits to him. The forbidden touch was completely overwhelming—hot, embarrassing, exciting. She shook her head and begged, "Take it out. Please, take it out."

"You are protesting too much, Princess. I think maybe you like the feel of my finger sliding past all these nerves. It's spectacular, isn't it?" he asked, gliding his finger in and out of her.

"Nooo," she wailed. She held her breath and tried to push his finger from her while she did her best not to notice how her body reacted to his touch. The sensations almost sizzled. Why was she so sensitive there? She bit her lip, struggling not to respond to his invasion.

"Don't bite your lip, Princess. I'll have to put something in your mouth to keep you from injuring that spot on your lip," he warned as he squeezed additional lubricant on his hand out of her line of sight. Her mental question about what he was doing was quickly answered as the size of the object squeezing into her bottom doubled as he inserted two fingers this time.

She released her lip to protest. "That's too much!"

"Not at all, Lalani. Bottoms have an incredible ability to stretch if given time and training. I will pay close attention to yours to make sure you are prepared."

"Ah!" The sound burst from her mouth as he widened his fingers apart and closed them, stretching that opening ring of muscles. She wiggled to get away from him and simply brushed her nipples against the woven material of the band around her torso. That thrilling sensation was like her whole body was betraying her. Everywhere she moved triggered an erotic touch. Lalani slumped back against the chair.

"Good girl. That's how you relax. Soon you'll push back against my fingers, asking me to fill your bottom."

"No, I won't."

He sniffed and raised one eyebrow, knowing she lied.

She watched him exchange the lubricant for the plug with his free hand. A small drop of the slick fluid oozed from the opening, capturing her attention. His fingers slid from her tight passage, and she looked up at him. A fraction of a second later, the cold metal plug pushed into her entrance.

"Relax, Princess."

She bit her lip and tightened her muscles to keep the

invader out. It didn't stop. Slowly the object stretched her entrance. Lalani moaned when the sensation became almost unbearable.

"You're fine. I promise," he said quietly. "Almost there. Don't clench those muscles. It makes it harder on you."

Seconds later, she felt the plug glide into her body and the outer guard settle against that sensitive opening. Lalani exhaled. She hadn't been aware she was holding her breath.

"Are you okay, Little One?" he asked, adjusting it slightly.

Lalani nodded. Overwhelmed by the feeling, she couldn't answer coherently. Each movement of the device inside her fueled her arousal.

Finally, he left it alone. "That's perfect. I'll be right back."

Lalani chewed on her mouth when he left the room. Was this the extent of her punishment, or was something else coming? He returned a few minutes later. Khadar stood by her side for a minute, scanning her body.

"You're biting on that lip again, Princess."

She stopped immediately. "Sorry."

"I've got something to help."

He disappeared behind her. She heard the slide of a drawer being pulled out and the crinkle of something plastic. Khadar rejoined her with something in his hand. "Open," he instructed, holding the object at her mouth.

Surprised, she automatically obeyed. When he slipped it between her lips, one section glided into her mouth. Lalani pushed it out with her tongue.

"None of that, Little One. This will keep you from injuring yourself." His finger brushed over her swollen lip, and she gasped slightly. It really was ouchy.

"You don't want this to become more painful, do you?"

"No," she whispered.

He showed her the adult-sized pacifier this time, rotating it in front of her, so she could see it. "I should have shown you this first. This fits in your mouth. You can suck on it if you get nervous, and it prevents your teeth from snagging that sore spot. Let's try it again."

This time, when he put it in her mouth, she tried it. She couldn't bite her lip. She felt silly, but his expression didn't change to amusement. He looked concerned. Tentatively, Lalani sucked on it. It tasted okay—kind of minty.

Khadar brushed her hair away from her face and smiled. "You are being so good. Let's see if we can wipe away all those black marks."

She nodded eagerly and waited to see what would follow. Khadar moved between her legs. He knelt. She squirmed, knowing she was completely exposed to his view.

"Gorgeous, Princess. We'll have to get a jeweled plug for your bottom when we have you stretched adequately. Something with a ring or a tassel I can tug. For now, you'll have to settle for a quick tap." He demonstrated by flicking the end of the plug extending out of her, jolting it inside her.

Lalani moaned around the pacifier in her mouth. She was so turned on. Should she be afraid or eager? Khadar demanded her total submission. And she loved his every touch. Her body responded with a gush of arousal, even as her mind struggled.

"That's good, isn't it? Let's see if Daddy can make it better."

He leaned forward to lick a path through the pink folds of her pussy. Instantly, her body teetered on the edge of a climax. Khadar sat back to look at her.

"Remember, this is a punishment. You are not to come

until given permission, Princess. I'll pause a minute to get yourself back under control."

When her body relaxed against the seat, he leaned forward again. This time, he spread her outer lips and concentrated on swirling his tongue around her clit. He never quite touched it but skirted around the small bundle of nerves. She tried to adjust her position to place herself directly under the path of his tongue, but her bonds held her securely in place.

Frustrated, Lalani pushed the pacifier from her mouth and begged, "Please. Let me come."

His mouth lifted from her body immediately. She watched him lick his lips, obviously enjoying her flavor. He stood to retrieve the object from the floor.

"Let me go wash that for you," he offered and disappeared.

She could hear her rough breath. He couldn't leave her like this. Need twisted inside her.

Returning a minute later, he flicked the water off the rubbery object and slid it back into place. "Keep this in your mouth, Lalani." His tone was stern. "Remember. This is your punishment. If you are very good, I might reward you later, but naughtiness will simply prolong your distress."

She shook her head. Lalani didn't like this. She hated this chair. "Never again," she vowed.

"Are you learning not to lie to Daddy?"

Lalani nodded. Maybe she could convince him that she'd already mastered that lesson.

"Good. Let's get back to your consequence."

He lowered between her legs once again. This time, it felt like his gaze was a physical touch as he looked over her body. A gush of fluid came from deep inside her.

"I love how wet you are for me, Princess. It almost makes me forget my purpose here, but I am a dragon. I have an incredible capacity to focus."

He leaned forward and breathed on her. The warm air brushed over her delicate tissues as effectively as a brush of his fingers. He tapped on the wooden chair support, and her breasts rubbed against the webbed restraint over them.

Lalani moaned as every inch of her flesh was hypersensitive. With each new caress, she felt more. Her attention narrowed to his touch.

Khadar pressed his mouth to her once again. Tracing her drenched opening with a featherlight caress, he thwarted her attempt to lift her pelvis toward him with additional pressure on her inner thighs. Just when she thought she'd lose her mind, Khadar thumped the plug in her bottom and sat back. Vibrations zinged through her. How could she be this turned on?

She panted around the device in her mouth, trying to regain control. Just as her body relaxed, he leaned forward again. This time, he pressed a finger barely into her pussy. He moved it slowly and shallowly as she struggled to pull it deeper inside her.

"You are so needy, Princess. I'm sorry you have so many Xs to erase with your punishment."

Her mind struggled to decipher his words. She could only focus on his touch. She needed to come. He had to let her come.

It took a second for her to realize he'd stopped once again. She lifted her head to look at him, pleading with her eyes. *Please!*

He tapped on the plug in her bottom once and then a second time. Following that, he gave a flick of his fingers that jostled the plug, driving it deeper while the guard pressed firmly against that nerve-rich entrance. The strong sensations were so hard to resist. Almost electric. A moan came from deep inside her.

"Let's see if you're really remorseful. Good girls can come from stimulation to their bottoms alone. Are you a good girl?" he asked.

*Yes!*

"I think you are too, mate. Show me."

He twisted the end of the plug and drew it partially out of her, making that tight entrance stretch. Just as he cleared the widest spot, Khadar reversed the process, challenging her to accept it. When it was seated fully inside her, he repeated the movement with a twist. Khadar added small pulses in and out on the plug's path.

Lalani attempted to bite her lip. The pacifier in her mouth stopped her, reminding her of its presence. She sucked on it frantically, trying to pull together all the tingles gathering around her. Her climax hovered outside her reach. She thrashed her head from side to side in frustration.

"Let Daddy help you," Khadar suggested and pulled the plug firmly from her body before thrusting it in fully.

Mind blown from the thrilling overload of sensations, Lalani froze, trying to breathe as he repeated that again. The plug drove past all those sensitive spots, putting her on the edge.

"Now, Princess," he ordered in a low voice rough with desire. He repeated his actions.

She couldn't disobey him. All that whirling pleasure fused together and slammed into her. The climax was unlike anything she'd ever felt before. Soul deep. Lalani screamed into the nursery, the pacifier falling to the ground as her body shook with the power of her orgasm.

Khadar clicked something on the chair and rotated her

body back to sitting up. He wrapped his arms around her and held her close. Dropping her head to his shoulder, she savored the pleasure he had awarded her.

"All bad marks erased. Such a good girl."

Lalani's lips curved in an exhausted smile.

## Chapter 11

Two weeks later, Khadar landed on the front lawn under the watchful eye of his mate. He always sent a message to her when he was almost home. Lalani ran to greet him as soon as he shifted into human form. She wrapped her arms around his neck and pulled him down for a sizzling kiss. He loved coming home to her. She was the most precious thing in his life. Khadar tried to show her that with every touch.

"Daddy! I missed you. Is everything okay in Wyvern?"

"It is. The crops are coming in to give us fresh vegetables." He gestured to the large bag he'd carried in his claw. "I think there might be a festival to celebrate the harvest."

"That sounds like fun. Can we go?"

"Of course. I brought some early tomatoes home so everyone could sample them. Would you like to walk with me?" He invited her, loving her eager cheerfulness.

After dropping some of the ripe produce off at the kitchen and getting a promise of BLTs for the evening meal, Khadar steered Lalani outside. He lifted the laden bag onto his back, using the handles like shoulder straps. "Let's go visiting."

She slipped her hand in his, and they set off on the path. Workers had always lived on his mountain. Many generations of treasured employees had passed along positions at his estate. After the change, a few more families moved to be closer to work. Khadar had assisted them with the construction of new homes. Having trusted workers close by was preferable to Khadar. He could protect them.

At each house, Lalani assisted him by retrieving tomatoes from the pack on his back and filling the arms of whoever opened the door. Everyone celebrated the early harvest and thanked them for the gift. As barriers closed, they heard other members of their families celebrating.

"You're good to your people," Lalani observed. "They enjoy working here."

"Their world just turned upside down. It's important they feel fulfilled and essential. I rely on my staff. Some have been with me for generations."

"Is it hard being old?" she asked before turning a delightful shade of pink.

Khadar laughed heartily. "It's okay, Princess. I know I've been around for a while."

"Sorry!"

"You are right. There are good and bad things about living for a long time. The dragon horde has survived thanks to the pact with Wyvern. With a mate, a dragon can withstand monumental challenges. Without a mate, it is easy to lose focus and purpose. Look! Here comes our housekeeper's husband."

After a brief conversation with him, Khadar shifted the bag to hang to one shoulder. "We're almost out of tomatoes, Princess. Our last stop is ahead."

"Do dragons have babies?"

"Are you thinking you want to lay an egg?" he teased.

"Dragon eggs are real?" she asked.

"Yes, Little One. Male dragons usually look for a female dragon to sire a replacement for themselves when they are near the end of their lives."

"Is it easy to find a female dragon?"

"No. They are very elusive. Rarely a female egg will be created as well as a male. Oldrik has a sister. They have not seen each other in centuries. If he knows where she is, he would take that information to his death."

"So, they're like a unicorn dragon," she observed with a bright smile as she skipped along with him.

"The most special of all dragons, definitely." Her positive outlook delighted him. He squeezed her hand, celebrating having her in his life. "I'm glad I found you, mate."

"I never would have considered having a dragon that shifts into a man as my love interest, but you're pretty special," she said with a laugh. "I do have something I want to talk to you about. I'm completely bored while you're off saving the world. Is there something I could do?"

"What would you like to do?" he asked.

"I worked as a hairstylist before. Do you think the people that live on the grounds would be interested in me cutting their hair? For free, of course."

Pride swelled inside him at his mate's suggestion. She wished to care for his people as well. "People will line up to get your services. What supplies do you need?"

"Some good scissors would be a great start. Clippers and other electronic devices wouldn't work any longer. Do you know if there's a beauty supply place in town?" Lalani asked.

"Totally not one of the things I focus on. Let's ask one of the staff people. There's one more house," Khadar told her.

A bright blue cheerful home stood surrounded by flowers. He watched her smile at the quaint scene it presented. "Who lives here?" she asked.

"Robbie!" Khadar greeted the large man who walked around the corner of the house as they approached.

"Khadar, what brings you on a walkabout? The last time you were here, you trampled my petunias," the man said. His friendly expression took any possible sting from his words. He was dressed in full sleeves and pants with hair that stuck out in all directions.

"I told you to leave a dragon landing zone," Khadar joked with him before turning to Lalani.

"Robbie, this is my mate, Lalani. She is new here to Wyvern."

"Hi, Lalani. I'm glad to meet you. I'm Khadar's beekeeper."

"Really? That's why we always have fresh honey on the table," Lalani said, and Khadar watched her mentally connect the dots. "You're a very good person to know. I have to admit, I have a sweet tooth."

"Nothing wrong with that." Robbie rubbed his belly. "I think I have a sweet stomach instead."

"We have tomatoes for you," Khadar informed him and shifted to remove the bag from his shoulder.

"Thank you. I'd heard the gardens were buzzing," Robbie said. Lalani rushed to hand him the tomatoes, so he took them.

Khadar noted she'd taken ownership of this job. He should have noticed earlier that she needed something to do. "Robbie, do you know if there is a beauty supply place in Wyvern? Lalani is a hairdresser. She suggested she could trim up everyone's hair around here if they needed a haircut."

"Put me at the top of the list. I whacked at the back

yesterday with scissors and made a mess," Robbie confessed, running a hand through his hair. "Wearing a netted hood to keep the bees away from my face is tough on any style but worse when my hair gets too long."

He looked away as if he was concentrating for a moment. "There is a shop in town. I think it's on Finegan Street toward the west end. I used to visit a curry restaurant near there from time to time."

"Thank you, Robbie. You'll be at the top of my list. If you have scissors, I could straighten your hair for you," Lalani suggested.

"I appreciate the offer, but I'm hot and sweaty from rounding up a new swarm. I'll come let you fix me up when I smell a bit better. I'll whisk these tomatoes in to savor with my dinner."

"Enjoy, Robbie," Khadar told him as he took Lalani's hand.

"See you soon, Robbie," Lalani said.

Khadar was pleased to hear how upbeat she sounded. As they returned to the house, he told her, "You can talk to me about anything, Princess. If something is bothering you, let me know."

"Could we go check if that shop is there?" Lalani asked.

"You bet. It's not far from a pizza place. They're still open because the pizza ovens are wood-fired," Khadar suggested.

Lalani almost bounced with excitement. "Pizza? Like real pizzeria pizza? Is it okay to miss dinner here? I think the cook had already planned BLTs."

"If we don't show up, they'll save us a few for tomorrow," Khadar assured her. "The cook has learned not to set anything on the table until I'm there. It's safer that way."

"Okay. Great! I'd give my left foot for a pizza," she confessed.

"I like both of your feet just where they are. What do you need from the house?"

"I just need to pee. Can I run behind that tree and go?"

Sensing it would take too long in her mind to get to the house, Khadar agreed as he schooled his face not to reveal his amusement. "I will wait here, Lalani."

He watched her disappear behind a clump of trees. His super-hearing could detect a soft whizzing sound that he'd never admit to her. Lalani would die from embarrassment.

"Ahhhh!" Lalani called as she tromped through the wooded area.

Khadar started toward her and controlled his expression as his mate tried to run, pull up her pants, and swat at a bumblebee at the same time. Khadar plucked her up and carried her a short distance to safety. He righted her clothes, asking, "Did you get stung?"

"No, Daddy. But she wanted to," she said, shaken.

"I'm sorry the bee scared you. You can have an extra helping of honey tomorrow just for spite."

"Yeah!" she said, nodding. Lalani instantly looked better.

"Would you still like to go into town?"

"Yes!"

"Let's fly, Princess."

In a few minutes, she settled onto his back with the ease of a frequent rider, and Khadar headed for town. He landed in a park a few blocks from where Robbie had described the shop. After shifting, he chatted with a few kids drawn to them in awe of his dragon before taking Lalani's hand and guiding her down the street.

"You're a nice guy," Lalani complimented him.

"Dragon."

"Sorry. You're a nice dragon. Talking to those teenagers made their day. I loved the 'when did you know you were a dragon' question. I think they were all hoping to wake up tomorrow and be a dragon."

"Of course, they were. Wouldn't everyone?"

"I don't want to be a dragon. Even if I'd be a dragon unicorn," Lalani said before grabbing his arm with her free hand. "Look, there it is. The door is open."

"Let's go get what you need. Let me enter first," Khadar ordered.

"Hello? Is there anything I can help you with?" a friendly voice asked as they walked in.

Khadar turned to see a teenager standing behind a counter at the front of the store. "Hi. My mate is a hairdresser and hoped to find some supplies to assist others with haircuts."

"That will bolster people's spirits so much. I've had a few people come in to grab stuff. I put the real treasures in the back so I'd have supplies for professionals like you. What's your favorite brand of scissors?" the clerk asked.

"I have some Equinox shears back home," Lalani said.

"Those are nice. I have a set of Kamisori Serenity scissors tucked away. Would those work for you?"

"You're kidding! Those scissors are so good they could almost cut by themselves," Lalani said, looking shocked. "I'm afraid I can't afford those."

"You can today. My parents own the store. They don't sell anything anymore. Just give things to people who need them. You're already assisting others by cutting hair. What else do you need? A cape? A sharpening kit for the scissors?"

"I'd love all of that. And a few hairbrushes and combs."

"You are a professional. The addiction is powerful for

brushes and combs. Here's a basket. Pick out what you need," the young woman said.

In a half hour, Khadar carried a bag filled with an assortment of supplies, including an old-fashioned straight razor, a lathering brush, and a pot of shaving soap. His mate had not been greedy but had taken what she would need and a few items that would allow her to give his staff an unexpected treat. He was very pleased and proud of her. Lalani had almost cried when the young woman had handed her the scissor set. She still held those close to her, as if afraid they'd get lost in the bag.

"Ready for pizza?" he asked, squeezing her hand to pull her from her thoughts.

"I can't believe she gave me these," Lalani repeated for the seventieth time. "They're so pretty, and they fit in my hand like... I don't know what they're like. These are so incredible."

"So, let's think of something we could do for the family that would be equally nice. I'll gather some information and see what they need."

"I would love that. Thank you, Khadar." She darted in front of him, making him come to a stop before rising on her tiptoes to kiss him.

"You are welcome, mate. Now let's go get dinner before I decide I want something else to eat."

"Khadar!" she said, turning a pretty shade of pink as she glanced around to see if anyone had overheard him.

"Daddy."

"Daddy," she whispered.

"Good girl. What do you like on pizza?"

"Cheese and anything else you prefer. There isn't a pizza I don't like," she said.

"So, I can have them load it up with spinach, black-eyed peas, and raw oysters?"

"You cannot like that stuff on a pizza," she told him with a expression of complete disgust on her face. "How about pepperoni, black olives, or even anchovies?"

"That does sound better," he agreed, steering her into the restaurant he trusted to provide a delicious meal for his mate. Food first. Then, perhaps, a snack for him later. Somehow his mate always inspired lascivious plans.

# Chapter 12

A picnic basket served as a perfect organizer for her supplies. With that draped over her arm, Lalani set off the next morning to catch Robbie at his house before the beekeeper headed out to tend to the hives. He was at the top of the list for steering her to that store.

"Be sure to tell everyone I'm cutting hair in the mornings on Tuesdays and Saturdays in the shade of the mountain. Right there in front of Khadar's house," she told Robbie when she was finished.

"I can't wait to show everyone. Thank you, Lalani. You're going to have a line a mile long," Robbie said.

"I may need to open more days then," she said.

"Start with two. We'll squeeze in during that time," he assured her.

"See you soon, Robbie."

As she approached the house, Lalani saw a gold flash in the sky. Drake was landing. And then a silver flash. Argenis was here too? What was going on? Her heart raced. It must be something tragic. Bursting into a run, Lalani raced toward the house, her picnic basket thumping her side as she hurried.

*Princess. Do not panic. Everything is fine. Your friends are here to visit you.*

Breathing a sigh of relief, she slowed her pace a bit and dropped into a walk before turning the corner. Aurora and Ciel waved enthusiastically when they spotted her.

"Hi!" Lalani called. She set her basket down to hug her friends.

"A little birdie told us you're a hairdresser," Ciel said.

"A birdie?" Lalani repeated.

"Okay, so it was a big, green dragon," Ciel admitted.

"And he didn't tell us. He told our Daddies," Aurora added.

"Oh, that makes sense. Do you need a haircut?"

Ciel blew a gust of air out of her mouth to ruffle her bangs. "These things are driving me nuts. I was going to chop them off myself, but I can't cut a straight line."

"Oh, I can do that easy," Lalani assured her.

"Could you trim mine up a bit?" Aurora asked hesitantly.

"Of course. Let's get a chair, and we can fix everything out here. It's beautiful in the shade," Lalani said.

"I brought some nail polish. I could do everyone's nails when you're finished, Lalani," Aurora offered.

"I'll do yours for you, Aurora," Ciel said. "This is fun. Like a spa day."

"What are our Daddies going to do?" Lalani asked.

"Dragon business," Aurora whispered loudly.

The three women glanced over at the clump of dragons, talking a short distance away, and laughed. They looked super serious as they discussed something important.

"Do you think they ever have a spa day?" Ciel asked.

Lalani turned her gaze back to the woman and shook her head. "I doubt that, but they seem to enjoy doing what they're doing."

"I'd guess collecting treasure would get old after a while. I mean, how many riches does one dragon need?" Aurora asked.

She gasped when all three dragons turned to glance her way.

Aurora quickly whispered to the others, "They couldn't have heard me, right?"

"Oh, they could have," Ciel said as the men came toward them.

Khadar stopped in front of her. "Lalani, we're going to look at something to the south of Wyvern. Will you be all right? Ask the staff for anything you would enjoy—snacks, drinks. Contact me if you need me."

"We'll be okay. We're going to have fun," Lalani assured him before rushing forward to give him a hug and a goodbye kiss.

When Lalani turned, she discovered the other women wrapped in their mates' arms. Smiling at the similarity between the three of them, she grabbed her basket and asked, "Could you bring a chair out here for me to cut hair before you go?"

"Of course. Want a stool or a kitchen chair?" Khadar asked.

"Oh, a high stool would be easier on my back."

He nodded and waved a hand at the others to let them know he'd return quickly. When he reappeared, Khadar set the stool under a tree and spread a blanket for them to sit on a short distance away.

"No pink hair allowed," Khadar growled at her.

"Really? You don't like colored hair?"

"Green's okay," he said.

"You. Go check out whatever has attracted your attention," Lalani said, grinning at his joke.

"Be good, Princess."

"Yes, Daddy."

They watched the men change and launch themselves into the air. It was a breathtaking sight to see the massive beasts soar into the clouds. When the three dragons had disappeared from view, the Littles turned to look at each other.

Lalani asked, "Who's first?"

"Me!" Ciel said, claiming the chair. "While you work, tell us all about yourself."

"And then, I have questions for you," Lalani confessed.

"Bring them on," Aurora encouraged her.

Later, with trimmed hair and fancy fingernails, the trio lounged on the blanket, enjoying one another's company.

"I can't believe neither of you knew about the dragons. Didn't you see them flying around?" Lalani asked.

"Not that I remember, but their eyes are so good they could have been way up in the air," Ciel said. "Besides, who's looking for dragons?"

"Good point."

"It makes Wyvern seem like such an important city. Do you think we're the only people with dragon protectors?" Lalani asked.

"Oh, no. Argenis helped a group connect with the dragons in their area. I met them when Argenis took me on an excursion. It was tense for a while. I think it was near Sarkany. Their forefathers had refused the pact. Argenis called the dragons, and one found his mate. It was magical to see her walk so confidently out of the trees to him," Ciel said.

"I've never been anything special. I don't drive men wild.

I sometimes wonder how I got chosen to be a mate," Lalani confessed.

"Me too," Aurora said, and Ciel echoed her.

"I've seen pictures of Argenis's former mates. There really isn't a type he goes for," Ciel said.

"That's interesting. I haven't even asked Khadar about his other mates. How old are Wyvern's dragons?" Lalani asked.

"You know that expression, older than dirt?" Aurora asked. When Lalani nodded, she continued, "They're not ancient, but according to Drake, they watched the mountain erupt from the ground."

"That's a long time ago," Lalani acknowledged.

"Did your Daddies share how the horde came together?" Ciel asked. "I've never asked Argenis."

Lalani shook her head.

"I don't have a clue," Aurora answered.

"Ladies? Would you like to have a picnic?" Louise, Khadar's housekeeper, appeared with a tray bearing glasses and a pitcher of tea. She was followed by her husband, who carried a much larger display of yummy treats.

"Louise, I'm so sorry. I stole your picnic basket, didn't I?" Lalani said.

"I never could get all the goodies, plates, and glasses in there. This works so much better." Louise dismissed her concern.

"Thank you, Louise," Ciel said, leaning forward to look at the trays as they set them on the blanket.

"Yes, thank you," Aurora echoed.

When they were alone again, Lalani tried a cracker. "These are good. Louise is experimenting with a variety of things. Khadar prefers to leave the supplies in the stores for those in the city."

"Do you think technology will ever work again?" Ciel asked.

"Life is so different now that you can't drive somewhere or have someone bring you stuff," Aurora said.

"I seem to have more time on my hands without a phone constantly demanding my attention. I didn't realize what an addiction it was," Lalani confessed.

"Neither did I. I still panic and look around asking, 'Where's my phone?' It's so silly," Ciel said.

"Everyone was tied to their devices," Aurora said. "What's the one thing you wished worked?"

"Oh, I'd have to think about that. The internet or TV, maybe?" Lalani suggested.

"Oh, I miss movies," Ciel chimed in.

"I'd say planes, but we have travel covered," Aurora said, laughing.

"We are lucky. I love flying on Khadar. Was anyone else scared the first time they rode on their mate?" Lalani asked.

"Drake's lucky I didn't strangle him," Aurora said and mimicked the choke hold she'd had with her arms tight around him.

"Does anyone get spanked?" Lalani blurted.

Aurora raised her hand, and Ciel followed a second later. "I bet they're all Daddy Doms. Who has a nursery?"

Everyone lifted their arms.

"Let me try one. Who has to take a nap?"

When their hands went up in the air again, the young women collapsed in laughter, rolling backward on the blanket.

"The worst part is Khadar's right. I'm exhausted and need a nap most days," Lalani said. "I don't tell him that, of course."

"Of course not. That's crazy talk," Aurora agreed. "Oh,

look! Here they come. Anyone want to bet they're here to fly us home?"

"Of course they are. I've had fun. Thanks for cutting my hair, Lalani. I don't feel like a shaggy dog anymore." Ciel ruffled her bangs.

"Yes, thank you," Aurora said. "I declare spa day was a success. We just need to have wine next time."

"Oh, we could have had that. I didn't think," Lalani apologized.

"We'll have to get permission first, or all our bottoms will be wine-colored," Ciel said.

"Let's avoid that," Lalani proposed as the dragons landed and shifted.

In a few minutes, the dragons collected their mates and flew off. Khadar stood with his arm around Lalani as she waved goodbye to her friends. When they disappeared from sight, Khadar squeezed her close.

"You like the other mates."

"They're the best friends I've ever had," Lalani answered truthfully. It seemed silly they could mean that much to her in such a short time, but the group was bonded. She missed them already.

"I'm glad. Nap time, Princess."

He looked at her with an arched brow when she started to laugh. That just made her giggle harder. Khadar didn't ask. He picked her up and boosted her over his shoulder.

Feeling daring, Lalani smacked his butt.

"That's an interesting way to ask for a spanking," he said.

Immediately, she backpedaled. "I was just playing. I don't want a spanking."

"Hmmm," he muttered. "Maybe those mates are a bad influence."

She gripped his waist and pushed herself up. "They aren't! They're my friends. Our spa day was so much fun."

"Hmmm."

When they reached the nursery, Khadar quickly undressed her. Lifting her into his arms, he headed for the large chair near the crib. With her cradled in his lap, Khadar pushed the rocker gently.

"Drink," he ordered, holding the sippy cup he kept next to the chair to her lips.

To get water into her mouth, she had to draw on the spout. It didn't automatically spill. The combination of his warmth, the rocking motion, and the sucking made her relax against him. A thought popped into her mind, and she pushed the drink lid out of her mouth.

"I'm not a baby," she told him grumpily.

"Is there something wrong with being my sweet Little Princess?" he asked, brushing the hair away from her face.

As she considered that, he inserted the spout back in her mouth and continued to glide back and forth. Lalani couldn't come up with any argument. She liked being his princess. It was a delight to be cuddled in his arms. Her negative worries dissolved, and Lalani slowly fell asleep.

## Chapter 13

Lalani woke up huddled in a ball. Her lower abdomen ached. She knew immediately her period had started. Sliding out of bed, she looked back to see a small spot on the crisp white sheet. She'd have to deal with that later.

She walked with her arms wrapped around her tummy to search Khadar's closet. She dragged her suitcase out from the corner where he'd tucked it and traced the claw marks on the hard shell.

"Mate, are you okay?" Khadar's bulk filled the doorway.

"No. I have bad cramps. I think I had a box of tampons in here," she told him, too uncomfortable to be embarrassed.

"Ah, Little One. Your suitcase is empty now. I have a spot in the bathroom for different products. Come, let me show you."

He helped her stand and guided her to the attached bathroom. Opening a closet door, he showed her a big assortment of pads and tampons. "Choose whatever works best for you. I had gathered some supplies in case I found my mate."

She looked at him in wonder. Khadar didn't shy away

from her needs—he'd actually planned for her. Lalani had enough for months. Relief flooded through her.

"Thank you, Khadar."

She grabbed a box and went into the toilet area to care for herself. When she came out, Khadar waited for her with a soft tunic that flowed over her body. Lalani rubbed her hand over the material.

"This is so nice."

"The package said it was like being wrapped in a cloud," Khadar said as he tilted open one of the mirrors in the bathroom to display some boxes and bottles of over-the-counter medicine.

"Do you want any pain medicine?"

"They don't work for me. I usually huddle with my heating pad for the first day. Then, I'm okay." Lalani shook her head sadly. "Without electricity, I guess that won't work from now on."

"I think I can help you with some heat," Khadar told her as he picked her up and carried her toward her nursery.

"I need to change the sheets," she said.

"Done. Let's see if we can make you more comfortable."

Khadar sat back in the rocker and held her in his arms. He lifted a hand away from her body and blew on it. Heat radiated from his body.

"Don't hurt yourself," she cried.

"Dragon."

He placed his hand on her lower abdomen. Gentle heat emitted from his palm. It was like having her own heating pad. Groaning in delight, she adjusted her new heat source slightly and relaxed against him.

"Heaven. Thank you, Khadar."

"Dragons have many uses, Princess. All you have to do is ask."

Overwhelmed by emotions and so thankful he was there to take care of her, she whispered, "I love you, Khadar."

"I love you, Lalani. You are my world."

Tilting her chin up, Khadar gave her a fierce kiss that demanded an equal response. Her discomfort faded from her mind as she tried to show him how much she loved him. A cramp pulled her away from his lips as she whimpered in pain. Khadar brushed her hair from her face and held her, not seemingly upset.

"Sorry," she whispered. "I'm sure you have a million things to do."

"Right now, I only need is tend to you." His soft kiss on her head didn't take away the pain, but it made her heart happy. He was here for her. She didn't doubt he always would be because... Dragon's mate.

A few days later, Khadar could tell his mate felt much better. She smiled and darted around at her normal energetic speed. Khadar made a mental note of her cycle. She wouldn't want him tracking her. That would embarrass his mate, but he was not bothered in the least.

Lalani enjoyed getting to know everyone during her haircut days. When she wasn't trimming away, she often accompanied him on flights or hung out with him in his study. She'd picked out a book from his shelves and devoured it, even after sharing she really didn't like to read.

Perhaps that was changing. She had chosen a murder mystery by a famous author who wrote in the early 1900s. He could hear her shocked inhales as the turns and twists were revealed as well as the quickening page flips as she got sucked into the story. There was no doubt she would try the rest from that writer. He would need to find more books to tempt her with when she finished that series.

"Daddy?"

Her question drew him from his thoughts. He looked up to find Lalani hovering in the doorway of his office. "Yes, Princess?"

"May I ride to Wyvern with the produce they're taking to the city market? I'd like to explore a bit and go visit my mother's home. I keep meaning to get back there."

"I'll be glad to go with you."

"No," she blurted. "I mean, I'd like to go explore on my own a bit. You're busy, and I don't want to rush. I'll just wander from the square to the house. It's not far."

He studied her face. "I would rather go with you, Lalani. I want you to be safe."

"I know. And thank you for being concerned about me. I'd just like some time to be normal—not a dragon's mate."

Inside, his dragon roared at the thought of her wishing to be something other than his mate.

"It's not that I don't love being with you, I just need some time to myself. If you're with me, I'll be worried about all the things you need to do. My plan is to choose one room at mom's house. I'll grab anything I think I should keep, then I'll contact you to come get me. Is that okay?" she asked nervously.

Khadar forced himself to answer calmly, even though inside his dragon paced and roared his disapproval. The beast feared his mate would be in danger without his protection. "I don't like you being off my mountain without me."

"Are you expecting something bad to happen? I need to be with my mom's stuff. I didn't get much time to spend with her. I'm intrigued to learn more."

"That is perfectly logical. I could come help you in a

couple of hours. You might have big boxes you'd like to have moved."

"I really just want to look around myself. I'll put anything aside that's too heavy. Promise."

He didn't like it, but what she was asking for made perfect sense. "Okay, Princess. Reach out to me at any time."

"Thanks, Daddy." She rushed forward to give him a kiss.

Before she could leave, he opened a drawer and pulled out three gold coins. "Put these in your pocket in case there's something you wish to buy downtown. The old government money is worthless now, but gold always has value."

"Oh, I don't..."

"I insist, Princess. I want you to have funds in your pocket in case of an emergency."

"Okay."

He could tell she thought he was crazy, but she accepted the coins to make him happy. Watching her ponytail swishing happily as she bounced out of the room, Khadar missed her immediately. He would be uneasy until she was back on his mountain.

Eager to go, Lalani checked to make sure she had the key. When she had everything she needed, Lalani went straight to where Khadar's workers were loading the first wagon.

"Khadar said I can go with you. He'll come pick me up later."

"He hasn't told me," the man said nervously.

Lalani knew he didn't want to get in trouble. "Really, it's okay. I'm going to my mother's house. It's just off the square."

"Oh," he said, relaxing.

She suspected he believed her mother was still alive and

there would be relatives to guard her. Lalani didn't say anything about her real purpose for visiting. After helping load a few lightweight boxes the workers let her move, she climbed up onto the seat next to the driver and held on as the cart lurched to a start.

The driver was a quiet man. After a couple of attempts to make conversation, Lalani started planning where to start. She had a strategy in mind when they arrived at the square. Sliding down from the seat, she thanked the driver and blended into the crowd before he could stop her.

Lalani explored the square for a few minutes and stopped to say hello to the huge stone dragon. He seemed friendlier than he had the first time she'd seen him on her mom's tour at the beginning of her visit. She looked at the steps and spotted Lalani Quintana freshly etched on one riser after the carvings for Ciel and Aurora's. Were all those other names mates? They had to be.

Mind blown, she wandered away from the square and toward her mother's place. Hers, now, she guessed. The house of the horrible neighbors was quiet next door. If only the Petersons hadn't been there after her mother's death. She greeted the man who'd promised Khadar to keep an eye on her house. He welcomed her back.

"Just here to visit."

With a wave, she let herself inside and closed the door behind her. Sadness washed over her. She ran her hand along the polished wood of the entryway table. Frowning, Lalani knew dust never would have gathered if her mother had been around. The photos displayed happy times. The last in the row featured her birth mother and Lalani.

She picked up the frame and pulled it to her chest, wishing she'd hugged the kind woman more freely when she'd been alive. Meeting her had seemed odd and uncomfortable, but in a short time, their interactions had become more natural. They'd just started learning about each other.

Placing the frame safely on the table, Lalani roamed through the other rooms in the house to make sure everything was okay. The air was stale inside, so she opened the back door to allow the breeze to come inside through the screen door. Upstairs, she pushed the window up in her mother's bedroom as well.

Lalani decided to start in the closet. She found a lightweight cardigan sweater that was worn with use where the clothes on the rack had been pushed apart. This must have been a favorite of her mother's. It was soft cotton and would go perfectly with jeans. Instantly, she decided to take that with her. She could wear it when she rode on Khadar. Folding it, she set it on the bed to remember to grab it on her way out.

Back in the closet, Lalani concentrated on the items stacked on the shelves and tucked under the clothes. She loved that her mother had so many shoes. Lalani had a slight shoe addiction herself. It was fun they had that in common.

Pulling a box from the very back, she carried it to the bed to open it in better light. Lalani pulled off the top and discovered two albums. She opened the first one and stared at a small baby alone in a hospital bassinet. In schoolgirl-precise lettering, her mother had labeled the child Lalani, royal child of heaven.

Her heart ached as she looked through the other items. The plastic ID bracelet bearing her name was stuck to the next page. The third page held a picture of her adoptive parents. It must have been attached to their application. The next page held a letter. It was written to Lalani in case they ever got to meet. Amazed by her mother's bravery and the love she professed for her child, Lalani couldn't imagine how she would have acted in that situation.

She wiped the tears away as they fell, reading her mother's assurances that she'd allowed Lalani to be adopted so she could have a good life. Small round marks blurred the page in different spots, and she knew her birth mother had cried writing it.

When Lalani flipped to the next page in the album. The rest of the sheets were blank until she got to the end. There, her mother had posted a printout of their emailed conversations.

Lalani closed the album and set it to the side. Flopping down on the bed, she allowed herself to mourn for them both. Thank goodness she'd gotten to meet her mother.

*Lalani? Are you okay?*

*I'm fine, Khadar. Just a bit emotional reading a letter in an album.*

*Do you need to return another day?*

*No. I'm fine. These are good emotions. I want to look around some more.*

*I understand, Princess. I will come get you at dark if I don't hear from you.*

*Thank you, Khadar.*

She put that album in the box with the other one, suspecting it was of family members. My family, she reminded herself. She'd take those with her as well. Pushing herself off the bed, Lalani headed back into the closet to find new treasures.

# Chapter 14

Lalani stopped and listened. Wood creaks sounded like footsteps downstairs and then again, a few minutes later, on the stairs. She shook off her silliness. All the houses in the historic area around the square were old. There were always squeaks in long-lived construction as the wood contracted and expanded.

She was on the last box. It was filled with legal and financial documents. Insurance policies, banking information, her mother's will. Most were worthless if the technology never returned. She'd hold on to it for now.

A quick look outside showed her it was late afternoon. Her stomach growled to remind her she missed lunch. Lalani decided to grab a quick bite of peanut butter and crackers before lugging everything downstairs and organizing it into something Khadar could grab to fly home.

She picked up one box she wanted to take, figuring she might as well carry it to the entryway. As she descended the stairs, the sunlight angled through the nearby windows and glinted on the entryway table. She could see her finger mark drawn in the dust. There was a clean circle in the middle, as if an object had been removed recently. She replayed her arrival, trying to remember what had sat in that spot.

The image of a silver candleholder popped into her mind. She remembered seeing it when she walked in today. It had just been there. Was there an intruder in the house?

"Hello? Is someone here?" she called bravely into what she hoped was empty space. Had a crook broken in to steal things that could be valuable?

No one answered.

*Khadar. Something's wrong. I think a thief is in the house with me.*

*Get out. Go to a neighbor's house.*

She nodded and then felt silly. He couldn't see her. Trying to be quiet on the last few steps, Lalani went slowly. The bottom step groaned noisily under her foot, and she froze.

A young man emerged from the kitchen. "You must be Loulou."

"Lalani," she said. "Who are you? Why are you here?"

"I'm just gathering a few items the neighbor owed us. Hopefully, we can pawn it in the next town," he told her openly.

"You're a neighbor?" she asked. That bit of information caught her attention. "You can't just claim other people's stuff," Lalani said indignantly.

"You can if they're dead. She doesn't need it."

"But they don't belong to you. You can't just help yourself."

*Lalani! Are you out of the house?*

*Not yet. There's a man stealing valuables here.*

*Get out!*

Khadar's tone made her step toward the door before her exasperation at the unmitigated gall of this man forced her to whirl back to face the burglar. She set the box in her hands on the narrow table with an angry thump. "You need to leave. There's a gigantic dragon on his way, and he's not going to be happy. You look crunchy—like a perfect dragon snack."

"Barbie Ann said you were a wimp in her note. She didn't add anything about a dragon," the man said nervously before he straightened. "Dragons sound like they're rich. I think I'll take you instead of the stuff. He'll pay a lot of money to get you back."

"Look, if all you want is money, you can have these." Lalani thrust her hand into her pocket and pulled out the three gold coins Khadar had sent with her.

"Yep. He has a lot of money. Come on. That's real justice. Your ransom will pay the smoke man to kill him."

The man rushed forward to grab Lalani's arm hard. She dropped to the floor, losing the coins as she tried to make it tougher for him to drag her anywhere. Her mind whirled inside her brain.

He dragged her toward the basement stairs. "Walk if you don't want me to bounce you down the stairs."

When she didn't move, he descended, pulling her after him. Her hip hit the first hard wooden stair, making Lalani gasp. "Wait. I'll stand up."

"Too late." He moved to the side of the staircase and flung his hand gripping her upper arm tightly toward the steps and let go. Lalani couldn't stop her momentum. She wrapped her arms around her head, trying to protect herself.

Those steps were brick hard as she bounced down wooden planks. Each whack into one felt like she'd break something. Lalani tumbled so fast, she didn't have time to dwell on any one injury. When she hit the concrete floor, Lalani rolled, knowing the pain would end. Focused on getting away, she let go of her head, and her skull rammed into the edge of a big metal appliance.

The edges of her vision went fuzzy. *Khadar!*

She didn't hear the roar that shook the houses in the city core.

Forced to land slowly by the people gathered in the street to figure out what was happening, Khadar thudded to the cobbled stones and changed as quickly as his bones would allow. He raced to the house and burst through the door.

"Lalani!"

Finding the gold coins scattered on the floor, he scanned the house, looking for clues. His emotions whirled inside him. Anger, worry, even panic tried to force him to act immediately. Khadar stopped to concentrate.

A sack with a silver candlestick spilling out of it filled the doorway to the family room. That wasn't how his mate would have packed things. The box on the table. Yes. That was hers. He searched the house and found nothing other than a folded piece of clothing, another container, and tissues.

When he got back downstairs, the neighbor from across the street stood in the entryway. He raised his hands to show he was harmless. "Can I help?"

"Keep everyone out," Khadar growled.

"That door there leads to the basement. It leads to a lower level," the neighbor said.

Khadar ripped the door open, tearing it away from the doorframe in his haste. Her scent hit him. He ran down the stairs and peered through the darkness. He could see the glint of green reflecting on different surfaces and knew his green eyes glowed due to his anger and worry.

When he spotted the small smear of blood on the dryer, he almost lost control to the dragon fuming inside him. Khadar forced his brain to think instead of rage. Boxes were shoved to the side, creating a path. Was he dragging her somewhere? He couldn't reach her mind.

Tracing the path, Khadar felt a faint waft of stale air. Zeroing in on it, he discovered an almost invisible door barely ajar. Wedged into the bottom was the bow he'd tied in Lalani's hair that morning.

He pulled at the door. It resisted his efforts but couldn't compete with the raging strength of a dragon, even in human form. As soon as the opening was big enough for him to squeeze through, Khadar dashed out. The path went both directions, with no markings anywhere that he could see.

Hesitating long enough to heat one hand, Khadar pressed it to the door to burn a print into the paint as he listened to hear which way he should go. A muffled curse sounded in the distance to his right. Khadar followed it.

When he thought he'd run past that sound, he stopped to listen. Nothing. He'd tear down every damn door if that was what it took. Fixing his eyes on the next door in the passageway, he dashed to it and rammed his shoulder into the barrier. It crumbled to shreds. He bashed those out of the way and invaded. A bullet zinged over his shoulder. That was the last aggravation he needed. The beast inside him seized control, forcing a shift.

"A fucking dragon!" the man yelled as he scrambled backward. Khadar's bulk pinned him to the wall, and crushed boxes scattered along the walls. The stairs in the center of the room were ripped from the upper doorway and smashed into smithereens.

*Where is she? Give me Lalani.*

The strength of his thoughts echoed in the man's mind.

Khadar did not feel a morsel of remorse when the man gripped his head like it was ready to explode.

"I'm here alone. I don't know Lalani." He gasped.

*What is this tunnel?*

"It was built long ago. It connects the original families."

How was he going to find her? Khadar wouldn't give up. *Why are you here?*

"I heard a commotion in the hall and cussing."

*Did you see what door he entered?*

The man shook his head. "No, I don't know. I'm sorry I shot you. All I knew was someone was breaking through the door. Only one person in each family was supposed to be aware of the passage."

He was wasting time. Khadar forced his heart rate to slow. There was no danger here. He needed to negotiate through the hallway. His dragon form would not work. Slowly, he resumed his smaller size.

"Send a message to my estate. I will have your door fixed," Khadar told the man as he hurried to the door.

"Do you want backup? I'll come with you. You could check all the doors faster." The man stood straight.

"I'll call for the others. They will come. Where are we?" Khadar asked.

The man rattled off his address, and Khadar sent it on to the dragons with a message asking for assistance in finding Lalani. "I'll open the door and send them to you. Are you going to the right? That's where I heard the sound."

Having lost enough time, Khadar dashed off, confirming right as he ran. Each door he discovered soon lay in splinters in front of him. He searched two homes, much to the surprise of the residents living there, before he heard voices coming in the hall. Familiar, gruff voices. Hope flooded through him.

Khadar joined the other dragons and rapidly brought

them up to speed. "Lalani was stolen from her mother's home this morning. She is hurt and not responding."

"We'll help." Drake jumped in. "We saw your mark on the door. Everyone, use a heat signal to show which houses we've cleared."

The next door popped open before they could get there. Instantly on edge, Khadar strode toward the older woman in the doorway. "Where is she?"

Her voice was shaky but brave. "I don't know, Khadar, the green dragon. The man who mistakenly shot you has sent runners to all the founding families with instructions to help locate your mate. The rest of the doors are open to you. Please come in and search so you can eliminate another house."

With a nod, Drake stepped forward to go through the house. When he disappeared, the woman said, "I never expected to see the gold dragon in my home."

"Do you have any suggestions for where I could find her?" Khadar asked.

"The families would never interfere between a mate and dragon. I suspected there would be trouble when it was reported that repairman, Aaron Peterson, was spotted," she reported.

"Peterson," Khadar growled.

"I agree. That whole family caused problems. It was a sad day in Wyvern when they purchased a house. Aaron didn't live with his relatives. Even he couldn't stand them. He has an apartment in the newer section of town to the east."

"You don't have his address, do you?" Khadar asked.

"I'm sorry." She shook her head. "I know it's in the Dragon's Arms complex. He shared that with the woman who allowed him to discover the tunnels. The last house that way is just on the edge of the old town. That's the place where Aaron found the entrance. The apartment complex is close."

"Thank you. What is your name?"

"I am Elenore of the Battlefield family."

"Thank you, Elenore."

"Go, Khadar. We will search the rest of the homes. You go on ahead to the Dragon's Arms. We will join you soon," Drake told him.

Khadar sped off down the passage, confident he was finally on the right course. The corridor ended when he reached the third door remaining in front of him. As Elenore promised, the homes stood open. A sobbing woman stood next to the entrance.

"He has her. It's that Peterson man. They went out the front. I'm so sorry I've caused all this," she called, waving to him.

Khadar sent a message to the dragons. *He's up on the street now.*

"He is evil. Not you," Khadar growled as he passed, thundering through the house and heading outside. Enraged, he held himself together with iron will, forcing himself to focus. *There!* He glimpsed a cart turning the corner up ahead.

His dragon burst forth in the narrow street between the houses. He heard his scales scrape against the stone walls as he leapt into the sky. Khadar covered the distance with one flap of his wings and landed in front of the cart. The spooked horse occupied the driver's attention as he tried to regain control. A scrawny man vaulted over the tailgate and dragged Lalani out. She tumbled to the ground, moaning as she struck the hard, cobbled brick street. Khadar's blood boiled, but protecting his mate overruled everything.

"Stay back. I can kill you with this." Aaron Peterson dug

a burlap-wrapped ball and a lighter from his pocket and held it menacingly like he would lob it toward Khadar.

"Don't do it, Khadar. It's the smoke bombs. He's been bragging about them. The only thing that can kill a dragon," Lalani called weakly.

Khadar hated the sound of pain in her voice. This brute had wounded his mate. He would die. Barely controlling the dragon's blood lust, he assured the beast that the man would suffer greatly.

Unable to use his sound for fear of killing his mate and the others around him, Khadar needed to keep him talking as he came up with a plan.

"Another Peterson," Khadar announced in a bored voice. "I thought I got rid of all your family."

"You tried."

"I wonder if they're still alive. If they were smart, they would've abandoned you here," Khadar commented easily as he sent calming assurances to the horse to prevent it from panicking and dragging the cart over his mate. Lalani had not yet gotten to her feet.

"They wouldn't have left me. As soon as this bitch is gone, I'll leave with stuff we can sell and live on in another town."

"You believe Barbie Ann is waiting for you? I only met her for a few minutes and figured she was totally focused on herself," Khadar said and watched Aaron take a couple of steps forward, away from his mate.

"You don't know her. Family is everything to the Petersons," Aaron answered indignantly, relighting the flame.

"Right."

Khadar spotted a blue dragon in the sky, and shortly after, the ground trembled under his feet. *Mate? Can you move? Shift backwards as far as you can without him seeing you.*

"I bet they've set themselves up in a new town as warlords. They're not even thinking about you. Aaron? Aaron who?" Khadar taunted him.

His heart broke as Lalani attempted to follow his instructions. She reached for bricks and wrapped her fingertips around the edges as she dragged herself away. Her pain ricocheted through his mind.

Oldrik stepped around the corner and assessed the situation. He moved toward Khadar's injured mate.

Aaron's eyes focused on something behind Khadar. Not falling for a trick, Khadar didn't shift his gaze as he used his senses to figure out what was approaching. Keres. If he'd ever wanted the black dragon close, this was the moment.

"You don't want to mess with him," Khadar informed Aaron.

"I'll just take all of you out. Then Wyvern will be open again," Aaron yelled.

"How do you think the citizens of Wyvern will respond if you eliminate the only creatures protecting them?" Khadar asked, watching Oldrik get closer to Lalani.

*Just a bit more, Princess.*

"They'll do anything we say. It took the Petersons to figure out how to kill dragons." Aaron boasted, holding his lighter ready.

"Dragons have always had predators. How much of that stuff do you have?" Khadar asked.

"What's the stuff?" Keres asked curiously.

"Dragon smoke," Aaron said proudly. "Or Dragons Smoked if you prefer."

Oldrik reached Lalani. As he picked her up, she cried

out. Either in pain from her injuries or from the touch of another dragon apart from her mate.

"Fuck! Put her down," Aaron said as he tried to keep all the dragons in view.

"Not happening," Oldrik stated firmly as he retreated quickly with Lalani cradled in his arms.

Khadar battled his dragon, outraged by the sight of his mate in Oldrik's arms. He redirected the anger to Aaron and released his dragon. Khadar sent a flame toward the man. When he dodged it, the packet in the man's hand caught fire. Could the flames destroy it before the bomb released its lethal smoke? He unleashed a second blast toward Aaron. Whatever happened, that man would burn.

A huge resounding ring filled the air. Everyone's gaze flew up to the gold dragon on the roof above them. The muscles bulged in the beast's powerful forearms as it dropped a huge iron cauldron.

Khadar's attention returned to Aaron. Everything moved in slow motion. The frenzied horse bolted, dragging the cart away. Khadar's flame raced toward Aaron. The first tendril of blue smoke rose from the packet as the metal kettle plummeted down. More smoke. The dragons moved away automatically, scenting the lethal concoction. Oldrik turned to run with Lalani, shielding her eyes as Aaron's clothing caught fire, and his mouth opened to scream.

*CLANG!* The immense cauldron engulfed Aaron, knocking him to the ground and embedding itself into the cobblestones. Drake's quick thinking had trapped the kidnapper inside.

The scream continued as Keres ran forward, shifting on the move. He directed his wings to blow the lingering scent of the smoke from all the horde members. The kettle trapped the rest of the lethal substance inside with the burning man.

Aaron's screams cut off abruptly as the metal around him heated to a glowing state from the flames inside.

"That can just stay there," Ardon suggested as he rounded the corner. Worried Wyvern citizens spilled onto the streets. He'd obviously held the crowd away from the danger.

Khadar's dragon roared, pacing forward toward Oldrik. Everyone scattered out of the way as the blue dragon set Lalani gently on the ground and retreated. Khadar looked at her crumpled body. His dragon was beyond distraught and wouldn't release control to his human form.

*Princess. Tell me you're okay.*

When she didn't answer, he roared at the crowd, keeping them back. A light touch on the dragon's paw made him look down. *Lalani.* Her hand caressed his scales.

*Stop scaring everyone, Daddy. Can we go home now?*

His dragon had never been more careful as he scooped her up in his claw. With a massive leap into the air, Khadar took to the sky. His mate would heal best on his mountain.

*I owe you.*

Drake spoke for the horde. *You would do the same for our mates.* His answer made Khadar roar in agreement. All mates were precious.

# Chapter 15

"Daddy?" One peek from under Lalani's eyelids assured her he was there. She admired the lush flowers and foliage before closing her eyes again with a delighted sigh. The beautiful sound of water cascaded nearby.

"Rest, Princess."

"You brought me to your favorite place," she said, waving her hand slowly in the cool water that surrounded her.

"This water soothes me when I am injured. I hoped it would help you as well." His voice rumbled over her.

Her mind scrambled to remember how she got here. She didn't remember anything between him picking her up in his claws and waking up now. She looked up at him. He supported her as she floated on the surface of the water.

"You needed to get his scent off me, didn't you?" she teased, remembering his outrage when she'd screamed at Oldrik's touch. The ear-ringing bellow had held a frightening threat that almost overshadowed the impact the other dragon's touch had inflicted on Lalani. "He was saving me."

"That's my job."

She kept her mouth from curving up in amusement at his tone. "You were busy flaming that jerk, Peterson."

"I don't believe you have any broken bones, Princess. Just way too many scrapes and scratches."

"I knew walking would help him get away faster. I pretended I couldn't move and collapsed every time he pulled me to my feet. That didn't prevent him from fleeing and dragging me behind. That outfit has to be ruined."

"Don't worry about your clothes. I burned them."

She stared at him.

"They smelled like another dragon and Peterson."

"Perfectly good reasons to torch innocent clothes," she teased.

"No one is allowed to touch you, mate."

"I should be prepared for caveman dragon behavior while you recover, hmmm?"

A few seconds passed before he admitted, "Yes."

"Noted. I don't think I want to be away from you for a while either. Besides, I'm going to be black and blue for days."

A low growl rumbled in his chest, and the water around them heated.

Lalani looped an arm around his neck and pulled him down for a kiss. She loved the flash of green in his eyes when he lifted his mouth from hers a few minutes later. "Chill, Daddy. You're going to boil the fish."

The heat flooding from his body stopped. She rewarded him with another kiss. "Good Dragon."

He looked so affronted Lalani couldn't help laughing at him. That didn't erase his expression.

"So—Sorry!" she said, trying to control her mirth.

"This is not a laughing matter, human. You could have been hurt or worse."

Sobering, she reached up to cup his clenching jaw. "I know. I'm sorry for worrying you. Hopefully, all the Petersons are out of Wyvern. They are bad news."

"You're never going out of my sight."

"How about we try with that for two weeks and then renegotiate? There will always be times you feel it's too dangerous to take me with you."

His stern expression eased a bit as he processed the truth in that statement.

To distract him, she lifted her hand in front of her face to examine the dragon pattern that had emerged at his first touch. It had a green tint to the marks now. A result of being in physical contact another dragon?

"Does it hurt?" he asked quietly.

"No. I felt a huge electric jolt when Oldrik picked me up," she confessed. "I guess it's reminding me who I belong to."

"Green looks good on you."

"It feels better inside me," she dared to suggest.

Heat flared in his gaze before he pulled back his arousal. "You are hurt, mate."

"I'm recovering with every second you're with me. Imagine what would happen if you made love to me," she suggested and stroked her hand over her shoulder to run between her breasts. She took a deep breath to lift her chest toward him.

"You are trying to tempt me, Princess," he growled.

"Exactly. Am I succeeding?" Feeling braver than she'd ever dared to be, Lalani trailed her fingers over her stomach, not paying an iota of attention to her rounded belly. She concentrated on the heat in his gaze. When her hand reached her mound, a rumbling warning emerged from deep inside Khadar.

Suddenly, the arm supporting her legs released her. As she tilted to stand in front of him, Khadar wrapped his arm around her waist to pull her flush against him.

"Oh! Did you burn your clothes too?"

"I do not wish to hurt you, Lalani." He ignored her joke.

"I'm not made of glass, Khadar. Remind me who my dragon is."

His eyes flashed green as he lifted her to bite the curve of her neck and shoulder. The slight pain skyrocketed her arousal, and Lalani's nails sank into his broad shoulders as her grip tightened. He boosted her higher as he tasted a path to press a kiss between her breasts. Turning his head, Khadar brushed the stubble on his cheeks over the sensitive flesh before capturing one nipple in his mouth.

She wrapped a hand around the back of his head to hold him close, silently asking for more. Understanding her need, Khadar pulled the tip deep into his warmth and brushed his tongue across it. She moaned with arousal, begging, "More. Please."

Shifting her in his arms, he turned his attention to her other breast and repeated this treatment. Errant thoughts eased from her mind as he forced her to focus on pleasure. He released one arm from around her waist, supporting her easily. Khadar stroked his free hand over her body, cupping her bottom.

Lalani wrapped her legs around his waist, grinding herself against his hard-muscled form. He slid his hand over her curves to trace the divide of her buttocks to the slickness gathering between her legs, despite the crystal water surrounding them.

"You are so wet, mate."

"Touch me. I need you."

"As I crave you, Princess," he said softly. He lowered her slightly in the water as his hand explored her heat.

She closed her eyes to savor the sensations but opened them to remind herself to focus on the present when a scary memory of her treatment popped into her mind. She'd felt so helpless and vulnerable as Aaron had dragged her away from the dragon she loved. Khadar's handsome face dominated her view, reassuring her.

He adjusted himself to fit against her opening and pressed her downward. His hips surged upward to fill her with his thick cock, as if unable to wait for her to engulf his shaft.

She gasped at the sensation as his shaft stretched her tight passage. When he stilled to give her time to adjust, she leaned forward to whisper into his ear, "Move. Now."

Instantly, he pulled out and thrust back in. Their bodies crashed together, straining to reconnect and bring each other as much pleasure as possible. He captured her lips, and his tongue slid inside to explore her mouth.

Lalani swirled her tongue around his, teasing and encouraging him as their bodies moved in an unrehearsed choreography. Buoyed and buffeted by the water around them, they celebrated being together.

Khadar ground the root of his cock against her, enhancing her excitement. She eagerly met each of his thrusts and caressed his hard muscles with an appreciative hand. Her fingers slid over his smooth, damp skin stretched over powerful muscles. Her arousal was fueled not only by his actions but by his breathtaking physique. The sight and feel of his form supporting her provided Lalani eye candy she'd never get tired of seeing.

Pleasure crashed over her, and Lalani ripped her mouth

from his to wail as he increased his pace, forcing every sensation possible from her body. She registered the flap and call of the birds startled from their perches, but nothing could take her focus from him. She tightened her muscles around him, loving the moan that spilled from his lips. It was a rush to know he responded to her as much as his caresses turned her on.

"Princess, you keep that up and I'm not going to last long," he growled into her ear.

"Dragons are allowed to have fun too. Let's see how fast I can make you lose control."

Her need to show him how much she cared for him made Lalani more daring than ever before. She didn't worry about moving wrong or touching him incorrectly. She simply let her body react to the one she loved. Bouncing against him, she stroked up her ribcage to offer her breasts to him. His darkening eyes glowed emerald green with a core of heat that sent a thrill through her.

The cool water around them provided a stark contrast to the sweat gathering on their bodies above the waterline. Lalani could feel all those sensations intertwining inside her. She was close.

"Come with me," she whispered as she moved on him, needing a climax like it was air for her lungs.

"Now!" he roared as he buried himself deep inside her. His mind forced their mental connection to the highest level to share his pleasure with her and greedily drew in her arousal to feed on.

As if he'd flipped a switch, Lalani's orgasm burst. Shaking from the sensations that buffeted her, she clung to Khadar as he emptied himself inside her. She had no idea where she ended and he began. Fused together, they shared the incredible gratification of their bodies and minds.

Later, when she regained touch with the real world around her, Khadar's fingers brushed the tears from her cheeks. She looked up at him in astonishment at what they'd just experienced together.

"I love you, Princess."

"I love you, Daddy."

# Chapter 16

With Lalani playing safely in her nursery with Ciel and Aurora, several members of the horde gathered in Khadar's library. Oldrik arrived after the scotch had already been poured.

"Started without me, huh?" the blue dragon asked. "I had to stop for some news."

"Are we going to like this information?" Khadar asked. He crossed to the decanter to splash a healthy amount of the amber fluid into a glass.

Oldrik made them wait until he sampled the drink. "Not shabby. The whiskey that is. The intelligence is serious."

"Out with it already," Keres growled.

His appearance at the door had surprised Khadar. The black dragon had always been reclusive. When the horde needed him, he was present, but to come to an almost social gathering was unheard of.

"Of course. I stopped at the chemist and received this report." Oldrik pulled a sheet of paper from his pocket and unfolded it. "These are the results from the chemist's analyst of the powder that, when ignited, has a negative effect on dragons."

"Did he have any luck figuring out what made you topsy-turvy?" Ardon asked, leaning forward.

"He was able to decode a grocery list of ingredients, even without all the useful machines that used to do this for us. Most of those are nonreactive ingredients usually added to bulk up a substance so it can be packaged. Some are the smoldering components to create the smoke."

"And?" Drake asked, arching an eyebrow as if he were waiting for the biggest piece of news.

"And three things the chemist couldn't determine. Those must be whatever affected me," Oldrik said.

"So, there's no way to determine the source and eliminate it?" Argenis asked.

"Unless you have some idea I haven't come up with. The first group of people can't answer questions, and the Peterson guy is roasted under a pot downtown," Oldrik commented. "There is one more thing. The mystery components wouldn't have to be dispersed in smoke. The chemist wondered if they would continue to try to distribute them in that way or if they'd switch to a powder or a liquid."

"Whoever made this was diabolical. What's the safest way to kill dragons? From a distance." Khadar answered his own question.

"It had a particular odor. Even though I was completely thrown for a loop, I captured that smell in my memory on reflex. Here." Oldrik pushed the memory out to the dragons' minds around him.

Everyone reeled back with a painful expression.

"Could you warn us first?" Ardon demanded.

"Just be glad you didn't have the extras that came along with that inhale," Oldrik said.

"So, we sniff everything?" Keres asked, shaking his head.

"That's a potent scent. You can identify it now," Drake said. "The Petersons. Are they completely out of Wyvern? Any lingering family members here?"

"The word at the passes is that each of them has turned away Barbie Ann, despite anything she tries to bribe them with. She's even tried to disguise herself and sneak in. It was brilliant, Keres, to mark them with permanent ink embedded in the cage bars you transported them in. Their black hands give them away at every crossing."

"A simple gift that keeps giving," Keres sneered.

"How many times do you think they washed their hands before they realized it wasn't coming off?" Khadar wondered.

"Oh, it will subside in a few years. Anything inked on the inside of your hands usually does," Keres admitted.

Drake cleared his throat. "The horde ruling over New York City has *collected* a number of subject matter specialists in an attempt to discover what caused the end of technology."

"The gathering was an involuntary activity?" Argenis guessed.

"Dragons don't ask for permission." Drake smiled. "New York dragons are a breed to themselves."

"Exactly. Did they share information with us?" Khadar asked.

"Only because there's no answer. They're expanding their search." Rogan strolled inside.

"And the red dragon joins us?" Khadar said, standing to welcome the newcomer. While dragons were a solitary breed, this peril continued to bring the horde in close proximity. He was territorial about his mountain, but he would do anything to protect his mate. "Scotch?"

"Thank you. I was delayed by the arrival of the red

dragon from New York. He just left," Rogan explained. He took the glass Khadar offered him.

"What does a New York dragon want? Wyvern isn't a bastion of scientific discovery," Keres pointed out.

"A mysterious colored cloud killed two of their own," Rogan explained.

"I don't like this," Oldrik muttered.

"Whatever caused the change, our purpose remains the same. Protect Wyvern. Guard our mates," Drake reminded them.

"And those to come," Ardon added, raising his glass.

One by one, the others lifted their tumblers into the air before drinking. The horde was in agreement. They would take advantage of any information, but their core objective was on the pact they'd signed so many years ago. Dragons didn't enter an agreement without committing to it.

A movement at the door drew Khadar's attention. Three mates were being naughty. He smiled as he lowered his glass. His mate had recovered now after her ordeal. He'd look forward to having her displayed over his thighs.

"Do you think they saw us?" Lalani worried when they made it back to the safety of her nursery.

"No way. Daddy would have called us out if he spotted me spying on them," Ciel assured her.

"They can't get mad. We have to find out what's going on," Aurora told them.

"Would you go back to how the world used to be?" Ciel asked.

"Me?" Aurora asked.

"Both of you," Ciel answered.

"Would I have met Khadar?" Lalani asked.

"Who knows? You would have been here for your birth mother. Maybe?" Ciel suggested.

"There were so many tools to help with tasks. I mean, how do you vacuum carpets now?" Lalani said.

"How important is that carpet?" Aurora asked perceptively.

"Not at all. Really, all I care about is Khadar. Even if the world was the same, it wouldn't feel like it after meeting my Daddy. Khadar would make it different," Lalani confessed.

Ciel nodded. "I feel that way about Argenis as well. He would ensure I'm happy and healthy, no matter if the floor was lava."

Immediately, Aurora crawled on top of the table. "The floor is lava?" she asked dramatically and waved the other women up to join her.

When they all balanced on the small table, Ciel said, "Our lives depend on rescuing Lettuce from the encroaching lava."

"Oh, no! Lettuce!" Lalani cried out. "How are we going to save him way over there?"

"I bet we can take these chairs and space them out so we can walk across the seats," Aurora suggested.

Ciel lifted one chair and set it as far away as she could step. When she successfully made the leap, Lalani scooted the chair from one of the sides in that direction. With helpful advice from the others, she negotiated her way to stand with Ciel before lugging her chair closer to the bed where Lettuce waited, looking scared.

"I'm coming, Lettuce," she promised.

"I'll bring the next chair," Aurora said and got busy.

They were all jumping on the bed, celebrating with Lettuce, when three dragons entered the room.

"No, your bed is not a trampoline, Princess." Khadar's deep voice brought the action to a halt.

"The floor is lava, Daddy. You're going to burn up!" Aurora cried.

The men simply crossed their arms over their chests.

"Maybe they're safe because they're dragons?" Lalani suggested.

"Dragons!" Ciel said and rolled her eyes so hard they practically made a sound.

A second passed as the women tried not to look at one another. Lalani slapped a hand over her mouth as reinforcement. Giggles escaped from Ciel's lips, and she collapsed on the bed, laughing so hard tears ran down her cheeks. Aurora was next.

"Stop! I'm going to wet my pants," Aurora demanded, obviously squeezing her thighs together.

Drake walked forward to pick her up. He looked toward Khadar.

"To the right, halfway down the hall." Khadar answered the silent question with directions to the restroom.

Drake walked out of the room with soft footsteps as if he didn't want to jar his mate into pottying, and Lalani lost it. Roaring with laughter, she dropped onto the bed. Her impetus onto the mattress made Ciel bounce up in the air. Her Daddy moved faster than Lalani thought was possible.

"Gotcha," he assured Ciel as he caught his mate. He tossed her over his shoulder and patted her bottom firmly—not a spank but a hard swat.

"Don't drop me, Daddy. The floor is lava," Ciel said, giggling happily. She didn't seem bothered in the least by his love tap.

"I'll escort this giggle bug home," Argenis told Khadar as he walked toward the door.

"Come here, Princess. Let's wave goodbye to your friends," Khadar suggested as he scooped Lalani into his arms.

"I can't go without saving Lettuce!" she protested.

Khadar rotated her body to hold her out sideways over the rumpled bed. He lowered her to grab Lettuce.

"Thanks, Daddy. The lava could have gotten him."

"Pfft! He's a dragon," Khadar said with a perfectly straight face as Aurora and her Daddy returned.

It took a couple of seconds for Lalani to process what he said. If Lettuce was a dragon and the lava didn't affect Khadar because he was a dragon, then...

"He was safe the whole time? We worked so hard to save him," Lalani said, then dissolved in laughter at their unnecessary labor of love.

Her giggles set off Ciel's and Aurora's once again. When they finally climbed up on their mates' backs, they were in control of their snickers unless they looked at each other. Drake and Argenis set off for their mountains, taking the long way around so they'd keep the two separated.

"That was a fun game, Daddy."

"I'm glad you had a good time with your friends. I believe I instructed you to stay in your nursery," he reminded her.

"I don't think you told me I was like locked in the nursery. We could go to the bathroom down the hallway, right?"

"It sounds like you're prepping me for a big excuse as to why you were listening at the library door. That's in the opposite direction of the bathroom," Khadar said.

She could tell nothing she made up was going to get her out of this. She tried tears. It wasn't hard to turn on the waterworks. Lalani just imagined how sore her bottom would be. Dashing her tears away with her fingers, she tried to look miserable.

"I'm sorry, Daddy. I didn't want to, but my guests needed to hear what was going on. It's not my fault. I had to be a good hostess, right?"

Khadar sniffed the air and smiled.

*Crap! He can smell a lie!*

# Chapter 17

"Can I come out of the corner yet, Daddy?"

"Have you heard the buzzer?"

"No."

Silence followed her answer. Lalani wanted to check over her shoulder so badly. Was he looking at her?

She could imagine the picture she presented. Naked from the waist down, Lalani somehow felt more exposed than if she was totally nude. Khadar required her to be in a certain position—her forearms braced on the wall to hold some of her weight and her bottom thrust out for his viewing. *My very red bottom.*

*Don't lie to dragons.*

"That is a very good thing to remember, Princess."

"I promise. I won't forget now. Can I come out of the corner?"

"When the buzzer goes off, Lalani. Not a second before."

She snorted unhappily. He knew she'd learned her lesson. He was just being mean. A squeak from the chair clued her in that he'd stood up. She felt his footsteps on the floorboards under her as he moved toward her.

Thinking he was coming to help her, Lalani pushed herself away from the wall, only to feel his large hand pinning her in place. She heard him rustling with something in a wrapper. Then the sound of something wet and thick squirting.

Lalani closed her eyes as two fingers of his free hand pressed into her bottom. She tried to clench her muscles, but he simply removed his fingers and delivered five sharp smacks to her bottom.

"Be good. I've already added five additional minutes on the buzzer. Two fingers could become three if you choose to continue being naughty."

The squirt of more lubricant made her freeze. "I'll be good. I'm sorry!"

Lalani tilted her bottom up.

"That's my Princess," he praised her as he spread the lubricant over her small entrance once again. She threw her head back as he thrust two large fingers into her bottom.

*I don't like this. I don't like this. I don't like this.*

"I don't believe you, Princess. I can feel you pulling my fingers deeper."

How could she forget he could hear her dramatic thoughts?

"Princess? Imagine if this were my cock filling every bit of space inside you."

Her attention rocketed back to him with that statement. To her astonishment, Khadar matched the movement of his hand to the sexy words emerging from his mouth.

"Here, Lalani. You like Daddy's touch here. Pushing over all those sensitive nerve endings. Being so naughty. Making you hot as I take your bottom."

She bit her lip, trying not to call out. She was so close.

When he removed his fingers from her bottom, Lalani blurted, "No!" and she turned to look at him.

"Corner!" he ordered.

"Oh!"

When she was again in position, he walked toward the door. "Naughty girls don't get to come, Princess. Stay where you are. I'll return soon."

She could hear water running somewhere. Trying to concentrate on regaining her control, Lalani inhaled slowly and deeply until her heart stopped thudding so quickly. The buzzer went off with a shrill sound that made her jump. She didn't look over her shoulder, determined to be good.

"Come, Princess. Let's get you cleaned up."

She jumped at the feel of his hand stroking over her spine. How had he gotten so close to her without her hearing?

"A bath, food, and some quiet time after all the shenanigans this morning," he suggested, helping her stand up after her corner punishment. "I like your friends. They are very imaginative."

"I like them too."

He guided her down the hallway and into his suite with the immense bathroom. When she was nestled in a warm tub, Lalani asked, "Do you think everything is finished with Barbie Ann?"

"Neither she, nor her family, can get to you here in Wyvern. I don't anticipate the passes being open to visitors soon. The change would have to reverse itself. Even if that happened, it would take a while for the world to readjust."

"It's not safe out there, is it?" Lalani asked sadly.

"There are sanctuaries scattered around where people have banded together—both for good and bad." Khadar knelt by the side of the tub and picked up a soft washcloth. He wet it in the water before smoothing it over her skin with rose-scented soap.

"That smells so good. Are there other places protected by dragons?"

"Yes. A few."

"Do they all have mates like here?" she asked, trying to be subtle.

"All dragons have mates. Are you asking if they're Daddies?" he checked, smiling at her.

"Yes. But I didn't want to pry."

"All creatures are wired differently. It's possible there are other hordes where the dragons are Daddy Doms. That is between that group and their mates," Khadar informed her solemnly.

"I can't believe I didn't know this existed. It's like there's a couple of worlds operating in the same space."

"We're very definitely from the same world. Humans simply chose a path to modern life that didn't include others."

Lalani rolled her eyes. "I guess we decided we were the alpha dogs."

They looked at each other for a split second, and she burst into laughter. "It's hard to be the most alpha species when there are dragons around."

"Truth." He helped her sit up so he could wash her back. Lalani moaned with delight as he stroked up and down her spine, erasing the tension caused by standing in the corner.

"Do you think all the technology will restart?" she asked a few minutes later when he had moved on to clean her feet.

"I don't know, Princess. It's doubtful if your scientists will ever figure out what happened: a solar flare, a horrible tech virus, a change here on earth, or something else. They'll keep investigating using the limited options available to them. Are you worrying about something?"

"No. The atmosphere is positive here in Wyvern. There might be a few people bemoaning the new situation, but most are taking steps to make life better. Having dragons helps. You all do so much."

"That is our job. To protect Wyvern. We benefit from our efforts. Come on, Lalani. Let me scoop my reward out of the tub."

When she was wrapped snugly in a towel, Lalani stepped forward and hugged Khadar hard.

"What is this for, Princess?" he asked, returning her embrace.

"I love you, Khadar. I can't imagine existing without you. Be careful out there, please."

"I love you, Lalani. Know that I will always expend my last bit of energy to return to you."

She nodded against his chest. Thank goodness it was hard to kill dragons.

Lalani squeezed her thighs together. She was still aroused from her punishment. His touch during her bath hadn't allowed her body to cool off.

"Daddy?" she asked, tracing her finger up his shoulder and across his broad chest. "I've been super good."

"You have, and I will remember that."

"But we could..." She let her voice trail off suggestively.

"Learning a lesson is hard, isn't it, Princess?"

"Yes. Totally not fun." She scuffed her foot on the floor.

"Would you like to go with me to pick up a couple of horses? They would probably love to interact with someone who doesn't smell like a dragon."

That changed the course of her thoughts. "I'd love that. What kind of horses are they? Are you going to pick them up with your claws? Will they stand in place for that? I'd run away."

"Come on, Ms. I Have a Million Questions. Let's get you dressed, and I'll share the details."

Lalani couldn't wait for the next adventure with her dragon mate. Who knew life could be so exciting?

## Chapter 18

Exploring her mother's house was a bit nerve-shattering the next time. Gone was the idea that this was a safe place. She'd returned alone, determined to be brave, but Lalani kept looking over her shoulder to see if someone had come in behind her. As a safe measure, she'd stacked a bunch of cans in front of the basement door that led to the passageway. That would at least give her a warning if someone came in. Hopefully.

She was there today to figure out what could be donated or shared from her birth mother's house. It had taken a while for her to be ready to sell this house or give it to someone who needed a place to live. There was no reason for it to sit empty.

Tackling the biggest job, she decided to start with the clothes in the closet. A big warehouse had opened on the outskirts of the town. They accepted clothing and furniture to pass on to Wyverns for free. Lalani would take her mother's clothes there for others to be able to wear.

A loud knock at the front door made her jump.
*Someone's at the door.*
*Be careful. Do you need me?*

*I'm sure it's okay.*

Psyching herself up to greet the visitor, Lalani crept down the stairs and tried to walk silently to the door. A loud creak announced her presence as she rose on her tiptoes to peek through the peephole.

"Lalani. I'm Elenore Battlefield. My family also descended from the founders of Wyvern. May I enter?"

Dropping to her heels, Lalani quickly unlocked and opened the door. An older woman stood on the doorstep. She carried a large tome in her arms. "I thought you might like to know more about your family."

Lalani's apprehension evaporated instantly. She didn't get any threatening vibes from this woman.

"I would love that. Will you come in? I'm afraid it's a bit dusty in here," Lalani apologized as she stepped inside to allow the woman to enter.

"No worries. Dust is eternal. It's either wafting in the air or decorating a surface. Your mother always kept her house so tidy. Can I put this down?"

"Sure." Lalani led her to the kitchen table and swiped her hand over it to clear the dust before standing back so Elenore could set the heavy book on the surface. "You were a friend of my mother?"

"Oh, yes. I knew Suzanne well. We spent a lot of time drinking coffee at this table," Elenore said.

"I wish I could offer you a cup."

"It's funny how the most insignificant pleasantries are the things we miss the most. A steaming cup of caffeine concocted with a push of a button. I mashed coffee beans with the bottom of a pan this morning to boil on the grill with my morning toast."

"And how was it?" Lalani asked, instantly drawn in by

the vivid picture that Elenore had shared. The two women settled into a chair at the table.

"Gritty. I need to find a filter or a mesh implement I can pour the water through. It was okay. I needed the caffeine."

"I understand that feeling." Lalani studied the enormous book in front of Elenore and asked, "What's that? Something to do with my family?"

"There's one of these around here somewhere. I'm sure Suzanne put it somewhere safe. We'll have to look for it to pass along to someone else in your family."

"I have family members still alive?" Lalani asked. Surprised by that idea, Lalani couldn't help but hope Elenore was right.

"Suzanne didn't share that she had a son with her husband? Those two never got along. Suzanne's husband and her son. I always thought it was a shame he didn't come back after his father passed."

"What's his name?" Lalani said, leaning forward in her chair.

"Oh, let me think. It's been a long time. I believe it was Derek? Yes, that's it, Derek Lowe. He left right after he graduated from high school. Jumped on his motorcycle one afternoon and never came back. Just like my grandson, Brooks."

She had a half brother? Lalani tried to remember the name Derek Lowe as Elenore kept talking.

As if understanding that one piece of information blew Lalani's mind, Elenore reached over and patted her hand. "Go write it down, Lalani. Derek Lowe. He was a handsome teenager. The girls went crazy over him. He would be older now, of course."

Lalani jumped up and opened a drawer. She remembered her mother had a notepad and pens there for messages.

Quickly, Lalani wrote out the name and the word half brother —like she would forget. It was so exciting to think he was out there. Looking at that line again, she deliberately crossed out the word half. The link with her mother was the most important—she didn't care that they had different fathers.

"Sorry. I'm a bit frazzled by that news. My mother never told me I had siblings. There aren't any photos here of a boy or teenager around the house."

"There was a bit of a scandal when he left. Suzanne's husband removed the pictures and virtually erased him from the family," Elenore explained. "Suzanne didn't feel he'd done anything wrong. She always thought the sun and moon rose just for him."

Lalani repeated the name in her head. Derek Lowe. He could tell her more about her mother. Elenore studied her, so she tried to drag her brain back to their conversation. Her visitor had said something about a grandson.

"Your grandson is out there somewhere? He didn't return to Wyvern?" Lalani asked. Her brows drew together in concern as she tried to pay attention to Elenore.

"It's okay. Brooks always does everything on his time. He'll get back here someday. When he's ready."

"I'd love to meet him."

"You'd like him. He's a charmer in a biker guy kind of way," Elenore said with a smile.

"I always liked the bad boys," Lalani confessed.

"Well, you certainly ended up with one. Mated to a dragon. You can't get much more *I'm not going to follow the rules, and I make the rules* than a dragon."

The two both laughed.

"Let me show you a few pages in this book. Then, if you would like, we can use it to find the location of your family's tome. They're all linked together. I'll show you," Elenore suggested.

"What do I do with it once we find it?"

"You hold on to it until Derek shows up," Elenore answered confidently.

"What if he doesn't come back?"

"A family has never ceased to exist up to this point. Even when major plagues or sickness hit. At least one person has continued the line. I'm going to hope a pact with the dragons somehow controls the future. He's going to return."

"I'm going to think that, too," Lalani stated positively.

"Perfect. Now, let me find a few items in here. You'll want to explore your book too. It has a lot about your family in it. Your family name is Morgan. So now you can read everything and pick out who your forefathers were."

"Morgan, hmmm. That makes sense that the women change names when they get married, and their children would have their spouse's family name. That really jumbles things up."

"Here's a list of the families. Look, there's Morgan."

"Henry Morgan helped create the pact," Lalani read out loud. A shiver went down her back. She'd thought her family was gone when her birth mother passed away. Now there was hope other family members existed.

*Are you happy, mate?*

*I am. Elenore is teaching me about my family.*

*This pleases me, Princess. I know how important family is to you. Listen to what she says. Ignore any message from your dragon mate.*

*Never. Love you.*

*I love you too, Lalani.*

"You have a strong bond to your mate," Elenore observed, somehow sensing Lalani was communicating with him.

"I have nothing to compare it to, but I do feel connected to him," Lalani shared.

"That is good. I hope you have many happy years together. Shall we take a minute and see if your family's book is here?"

"I haven't run into it. You said they were connected. How?"

Elenore closed her book carefully so she didn't tear or bend any pictures. She placed her right hand on the cover and rubbed a counterclockwise circle on the embossed leather.

Lalani leaned in. "Is it glowing?"

"You're very perceptive. Not everyone can see that. Now watch." Elenore stood and walked toward the rear of the house. The light dimmed.

"Not in that direction," Elenore stated firmly and turned to stroll into the center of the house. At each possible turn, she consulted the book's glow. The light was unmistakable when she reached the cabinet under the TV.

"Can we check here?" Elenore asked, looking at Lalani, who stood beside her.

"Of course. Let me do it."

She dropped to her knees and opened the doors. It was illuminated as if electricity fueled a bulb inside. Lalani moved a few things collected inside and found it. The huge tome.

Pulling it out, she stood and placed it next to Elenore's. The light was almost blinding. "That's unbelievable."

"You can extinguish it. Simply rub a clockwise pattern on the cover." Elenore demonstrated, and Lalani watched with amazement as it became a simple book once again.

"Take that with you. If you have questions, I'm always glad to answer them. When another Morgan appears, you will pass that on to them. Mates are not the keepers of a family's tome."

"Could I ask about the tunnels? Why are some houses linked?" Lalani asked.

"Creating the pact with the dragons forged a common bond between the founding families. While they have supported all those who settled in Wyvern, the dragons have viewed those descending from the first settlers as their most important allies. In recent years, the keepers of these tomes have worked together to educate one another, for frequently the books have passed to someone who knew nothing about the pact or dragons."

"Like me," Lalani said, looking at the thick volume in her hand. "I'll never make it through all of this. Is there like a cheater study guide?"

"There is not. I've had the book for twenty years, and I haven't gotten through all of it. You have to read and think. Then go back for another chunk. My grandmother passed along the list of parts she suggested were the most important. It helped me. I've copied it for you and added a suggestion of my own that you should start with," Elenore said, pulling a handwritten sheet from the book and handing it over.

"Thank you so much. I wonder if my mother had a note like this?" She opened the top cover, and an outline floated down to the ground.

"Looks like you're in luck," Elenore said with a smile. "I bet they all decided to do the same thing. It sounds like something they would have planned together."

"I think this is in my mother's handwriting." Lalani smiled at the paper. It had just become the most treasured item she had.

"She'd be so glad you have it. Your mother mentioned you frequently. How old you would be. When it was your birthday. How she hoped for the best of everything for you. And how she dreamed that when you were an adult you would come to find her."

Tears coursed down Lalani's face. She set the book on a table and grabbed a few tissues from the box. "Could you tell me more about my mother?"

"I would love to. We can discuss the book and your mom. Let me show you this first. Here are the stories of the first mates." Elenore pointed to the top item on both lists. "You're going to love these profiles. Then go look at the steps in the town square."

Lalani impulsively stepped forward to hug Elenore. "Thank you for coming. I can't wait to get to know you as well."

"If you'd like, I'll introduce you to the others. They'll be thrilled to meet the green dragon's mate."

"I'd like that. Thank you." What an amazing visit! She had a brother, a place in the history of Wyvern, a new friend who'd known her mother well, and so much to learn. Lalani couldn't wait to discover more.

# Chapter 19

Just as Elenore had suggested, Lalani devoured the section about the first mates. All such amazingly different stories about incredibly brave women. When Khadar had announced they would attend the harvest festival, Lalani planned to visit the mates' stairway.

Now, standing at the bottom of the steps, she picked out the names carved on the bottom step. Incredible, strong people who allowed themselves to love a dragon. Their dragon mate.

"You are staring so hard. Is everything okay, Princess?" Khadar asked, wrapping his arm around her waist.

"The book brought these ladies alive for me. Seeing this now means so much more than before," she said.

"They aren't a set of letters anymore. They're people," he suggested.

"That's it exactly. Your initial mate was Brigitte O'Neil." Lalani pointed to her name. "You met picking berries by the river." She studied Khadar's face, trying to gauge his emotions. It was hard to know that he'd loved others.

"She was gathering fruit. I was cleaning the blood off my

scales from a battle. Brigitte did not like violence. She was a peaceful woman."

"What did you think when she didn't run?" Lalani asked.

"Her scent had lured me there. The bath was an attempt to not turn her off completely. Brigitte proceeded to lecture me about the need for talking before fighting."

"Didn't you have to kill some of the people that attacked you?" Lalani asked.

"Yes. She shouldn't have been out there alone. It wasn't safe. I took care of the problem quickly. In the aftermath, Brigitte decided maybe having a dragon around was okay," Khadar said with a laugh.

"It was a violent time back then."

"It was. Surviving was difficult for humans. Between diseases and lack of medical knowledge, many didn't survive to see forty. Especially women. Brigitte was my mate for over a hundred years."

"How long do you think I'll live?" Lalani asked.

"My heart says forever. The future is never sure. We'll enjoy every minute together, Princess."

She smiled and opened her mouth to celebrate that idea with him when hands clasped over her eyes. With Khadar there, it had to be someone safe, so she didn't panic.

"Guess who?"

"Aurora?" she guessed, deliberately choosing the wrong mate.

"Aurora? Do I sound like this?" Ciel launched into a description of the epic party on the square in the exact tone their friend would have spoken.

"That's amazing, Ciel. I knew it was you," Lalani revealed as she turned around to hug her friend.

"She imitates me well, doesn't she?" Aurora said, stepping forward to get her hug as well.

"She could be a perfect copycat. You probably could have made millions on scam calls," Lalani suggested.

"Too bad there aren't any phones. There's one job possibility tanked now," Ciel joked.

"The watermelon contest is next. Let's go watch," Aurora suggested.

"That sounds like fun," Lalani agreed. She looked up at Khadar for permission.

"Go, Princess. Stay with the group."

"Yes, sir!" Lalani answered, snapping to attention and saluting.

"Oh, you're going to get in trouble for that one," Ciel whispered as they hurried away.

"Maybe he'll forget," Lalani said, crossing her fingers, already regretting her mocking movement.

"Dragons never forget," Aurora reminded her.

They joined the crowd, standing in front of the long tables set together. Fifteen contestants stood behind the tables with their hands clasped behind their backs. In front of each person sat a large watermelon wedge.

Lalani couldn't help but compare being at this gathering today versus when the guards had carted her in before. She was a Wyvern now. This was where she belonged.

"Who talked Ardon into participating?" Lalani asked, staring at the immense man who looked like he could eat the whole thing, rind and all, in a bite.

"He lost a bet with Oldrik," Ciel explained.

"Those other contestants don't seem happy to be competing against a dragon, even in human form," Aurora said.

The whistle blew, starting the watermelon-eating challenge, just as an enormous shadow passed over the area. People scrambled out of the dragon landing area as the black dragon dropped to the earth. Trapped in his claws were two men who cursed like sailors while a woman clung to his neck with desperate determination.

Ardon ran off the stage and toward Keres. Lalani hooked her arms with Ciel and Aurora and towed them over to find out what was going on. As soon as the woman slid to the ground, Keres shifted and captured the men by their collars.

"Caught these two sneaking over the border," Keres announced, shaking the men slightly.

"You didn't just drop them a few miles away?" Drake asked.

"The border people vouched for them. One is part of the founding family that gave us Khadar's mate," Keres explained.

"Derek Lowe?" Lalani said, stepping away from the others.

A man a few years younger than her turned to grin at her. "I see my reputation as a ladykiller is still active in Wyvern."

Lalani had to laugh at his rakish smile. "I don't know about that, but I just found out my birth mother had a son named Derek Lowe."

"You couldn't be Lalani?" he guessed, shrugging off Keres's grasp and walking toward her.

"Suzanne told you about me?" Lalani asked. Knowing her mother had talked about her and kept her memory close made Lalani feel cherished.

"Your name was on an ornament on our Christmas tree every year. And I loved celebrating your birthday. Cake is important to kids. Your birthday was a fun day. I still remember it, March twenty-sixth."

"That's amazing. Our mother was amazing." Tears coursed down her cheeks, and she didn't even try to wipe them away. She felt Khadar's presence behind her and leaned against his hard form to let him support her.

"You're a dragon's mate?" Derek said as his eyes widened in shock.

"This is Khadar." Lalani introduced him.

The man and shifter nodded a greeting as they silently sized each other up.

"Can I give you a hug?" Lalani asked.

"Whenever we see each other from now on. We have lots of time to make up," Derek said, stepping forward to hold out his arms. He squeezed her tightly before releasing her and stepping back.

"Did I hear you say our mother *was* amazing?" he asked, emphasizing the past tense she used.

"I'm sorry. You probably hadn't heard. She was killed in an accident just after I came to visit. Did you know your dad is gone too?"

"Yes, friends clued me in. I thought about returning then but figured I'd been gone too long already. That was a mistake. I never considered I wouldn't get to see Mom again."

"I'm glad you're here now. The dragons ensure Wyvern is safe."

"It's taken me a while to get here. The world is crazy out there. Being picked up by a dragon wasn't anything I expected to experience today."

"I'm sure Keres didn't explain," Lalani said, looking over her shoulder at Khadar. "Who's the other man?"

"That guy and I found each other about two hundred miles from here as we both tried to get the last bottle of Pappy Van Winkle, the finest bourbon around. We decided to both enjoy it together and discovered we had more than a common love of aged whiskey. He's from Wyvern too."

"Brooks? Oh, good heavens. Is that you?"

Lalani turned at the sound of her friend's voice. Elenore rushed toward the other man, who immediately shrugged out of the leather jacket Keres had him trapped by. He ran to wrap his arms around the older woman and turned in a happy circle. Lalani's heart swelled with happiness. She knew how much Brooks meant to Elenore.

"Grandma!"

"You've been traveling with Brooks Battlefield?" she asked Derek.

"Yep. We recognized each other's names as we talked. It seemed like a good idea that two men from Wyvern should stick together. I don't think either of us would have gotten home alone."

"We have a lot of catching up to do," Lalani said.

A movement in the sky caught her attention. She whirled to see Oldrik land and shift. He seemed to sniff the air and strode toward Keres and the young woman.

"Who's the woman?" Lalani asked.

"That's Skye. We saved her from a bunch of thugs. It's not safe for anyone to be by themselves, but women are an easy target," Derek told her quietly. "She doesn't speak much. We don't know exactly what she went through before we found her. Somehow, we earned her trust and kept her with us."

"There's no way she's from Wyvern too," Khadar said.

"There is actually. That and home are the only words we've heard her say. She chimed in with both when we were talking about people we remembered back here. We brought her with us. She's one hell of an artist. We left incredible drawings of dragons everywhere we stopped."

"I'd guess she was Oldrik's mate from his reaction, but he's leaving," Khadar said. "Ardon is there now."

The younger dragon repeated that same sniffing motion as he strode forward. She focused on eavesdropping.

"Introduce me," Ardon demanded of Keres as he stopped in front of the black dragon.

"I'll tell you the same thing I told Oldrik. I don't know her," Keres said, shaking his head.

"What is your name, Little One?" Ardon asked.

"Skye," she whispered, facing the crowd for the first time.

Ardon stared at the young woman as if trying to figure out a puzzle missing a vital piece.

"Skye? Is that you? Please, let me through. That's my daughter," a woman called from the assembly as she pushed her way from behind the crowd. Immediately, an aisle formed for her.

Ardon eased back as the worried mother ran forward to wrap her arms around the new arrival. "I'm so glad to see you. A dragon visited the art college to collect you, but you'd already left."

"Hi, Mom."

"Let's get you home. You need a bath and something to eat."

"There are dragons here, Mom. I need paper. I want to sketch them."

"You can draw dragons later, Skye."

"No, Mom. I need to capture them now," Skye stressed. "It's important."

"You don't even have paper, Skye. Don't be silly. Come to the house with me."

"I have that paper I brought to make a pencil rubbing of the names. I'll be right back," Lalani told Khadar. Something told her this was important. When he nodded, she rushed forward, opening the tote bag draped over her shoulder.

"Hi. I'm Lalani. I couldn't help overhearing. Would this

work for you?" Lalani said, offering the sketch pad. "I have pencils, too."

"Thank you." The grateful look on Skye's face told her everything. Lalani remembered both Ardon and Oldrik's reactions to her. Was she one of their mates?

As the woman sat down on the grass to open the pad, Ardon shifted into dragon form. He stood as still as a statue as Skye put the tip of her pencil on the blank page.

*This is going to be fun to watch.*

*Mate, do not interfere in the affairs of dragons.*

*I'd never do that.* Lalani crossed her fingers behind her back as she lied. Something was going on. She couldn't wait to find out what happened next.

Thank you for reading Khadar: Fated Dragon Daddies 3!

Don't miss future sweet and steamy Daddy stories by Pepper North? Subscribe to my newsletter!

I'm excited to offer you a glimpse into The Magic Of Twelve: Violet. Readers Beware: The Magic of Twelve Series is intended to leave the audience enchanted and wanting more. Each of these fantastical love stories features sizzling scenes that may leave the reader as uncomfortable as the heroine's bottom. Tread carefully with the Sorcerers of Bairn if you are sensitive to high heat.

5.0 out of 5 stars
**Excellent story!**
Pepper North has such a way of telling stories. Her kindness and caring with the characters is amazing. I have been

reading her books for a while and I always come back to read them over and over. This story was wonderful and humorous. With just enough suspense to keep you on the edge of your seat and a beautiful ending.

5.0 out of 5 stars
**A very unique story concept!**
This book was a lot of fun! Very unique from any romance and any age play books I've read before. It was a blend of both of those things AND sorcery/magic. Very unique.

This set up the series fantastically and I can't wait to see how things unfold. But what I'm really excited for is to see what happens after all 12 woman are with their sorcerer daddies.

I enjoyed Violet's rebellious/defiant streak. Those are always my favorite types of characters to read, those that are strong willed and strong minded. Gotta give that Pappa a run for his money! 😉

## The Magic Of Twelve: Violet
## Chapter One

Violet DuMass dropped her purse on the entryway table and shrugged her coat from her shoulders. She was a little tipsy from the happy hour margarita that she had enjoyed with a group of colleagues after work to celebrate her twenty-second birthday. Turning, Violet double-checked that the deadbolt on the door was locked. Her shoulders sagged a little in relief. She'd had a strange feeling that someone had been watching her today. She kept looking over her shoulder and around the office building, but she never caught anyone looking at her strangely.

Breathing a sigh of relief, she walked down the hall unbuttoning the pale pink blouse her mother had sent her for her birthday. It was one of the only clothing presents she had ever received from her mother that she would actually wear. *Maybe her taste is improving.* Violet laughed at the thought. As she approached her bedroom door, she reached down and pulled off her high heels. Wiggling her toes in relief, she walked into her room and put the heels in her closet.

Something caught her eye. A strange fluttering motion seemed to ripple in the antique mirror that she had brought with her when she moved out of her parents' home. She'd always loved the gilt frame that encircled it. Heavens knows as a teenager she'd spent enough time peering into it, hoping to magically be transformed into a ravishing beauty.

As she walked forward to look closer, Violet saw her reflection. Still no ravishing beauty, but she considered herself nice to look at with long, deep brown hair and the eye-catching violet eyes that had inspired her name. Her lips were full and usually smiled with an enjoyment of life. She brushed her bangs out of her eyes and leaned closer.

There! There it was again. It looked like a butterfly was trying to flutter its way through the mirror. Violet reached a tentative hand up to the mirror and touched the cool surface. A dramatic flash of light burst around her, and Violet felt herself being pulled forcefully through the mirrored surface.

She tumbled forward and pressed her shaking hands against a sparkling white marble floor. Glancing up in confusion, Violet scrambled to her bare feet and looked around in shock. This was not her apartment. She clutched the front of her blouse together in her hands. She was in a large room decorated as if it was a receiving chamber in a medieval Italian palace. Turning, she saw the twin of her mirror hanging behind her on the wall. She raced back to it, slapping her hands frantically to the cold surface. It was solid. She ran her fingers along the sides of the heavy frame but found nothing. Violet turned shaking to press her back against the wall. She had taken a self-defense class last year, and she remembered the instructor stressing that this was the only way to be safe from at least one side. It was also a good way to get trapped, but she wasn't going to think about that possibility.

Looking around the area, Violet was bewildered. The room she was in had a mixture of old, new, and weird items all gathered together. In the corner was a desk with a laptop computer but over in front of the lighted panel was an old-fashioned spyglass. There was a cabinet on the opposite wall filled with antique apothecary jars and vials.

"Where am I?" Violet whispered to herself just to hear her own voice and know that she was awake. "What did they put in that margarita?"

A deep voice came from the arched doorway to her right. "I wondered when you would arrive. It is 7:23, one minute after your birth, twenty-two years ago." She twisted her neck quickly to look at him. He was massive, at least seven feet tall with a wide chest and shoulders. A black beard and mustache covered the lower third of his face. His shiny black hair was braided intricately down the back of his head, and the tail of the braid lay thick and heavy over his shoulder. Dangling from his left ear was a polished, intricate steel earring.

"Ummmm, I'm not sure where I am. There must have been some mistake. I know this is going to sound crazy, but I just touched the surface of my old mirror and . . ." Violet attempted to explain.

"And you fell through the mirror, landing here in my study," he completed easily. "Welcome to your new life," he said dryly. "I have been waiting for you to become an adult and come to me for many years, Violet. Now, let's get you settled in," the man began as he waved his hand in an intricate pattern through the air.

Violet felt her clothes begin to slide from her body. She attempted to hold on to each piece, but they slipped through her fingers. Finally, she stood in front of the strange man wearing only her white lace bra and panties. Wrapping her arms around her torso to shield herself from his view, Violet blustered, "I don't know how you did that, but you have no right to take my clothing, sir. Give them back immediately. Who do you think you are?"

With a casual wave of his hand, her arms straightened and froze by her sides. "Your old clothes are no longer necessary for you. You're not in Atlanta anymore. Here, I decide what you wear or don't wear." He flicked his fingers, and her bra and underwear disappeared.

Using all her strength, Violet strained to cover herself, but she was held solidly in place. She opened her mouth to scream but found her lips sealed together. "Aarrrrggghhhh!" the muffled sound stilled in her throat. She watched in horror as the man approached her silently stopping several feet away. His ice-blue eyes ranging over her exposed body as he gestured once again, and her feet slid across the floor to stop in front of him.

"I am Garrick. You were matched with me twenty-two years ago. I'm assuming your earth government has not revealed its agreement to allow the collection of children who are the destined ones for the Sorcerers of Bairn?" He chuckled at the look in her eyes. He waved a finger releasing her mouth to speak.

"Are you mad? There isn't any Earth government. There are separate countries all over Earth that make their own rules and treaties. And really? The Sorcerers of Bairn? I can't think of anything that sounds more made up! Maybe the term destined ones!" indignant words burst from her mouth before once again with a finger movement her lips were sealed. "Aarrrrggghhhh!"

"Now, I can see why your destiny completes mine. Your form is beautiful, but your fire and spirit will keep me on my toes for a millennium. Since you have amused me, I will answer your questions. The leaders of each country on Earth were gathered at the great hall. Each decided to sign the agreement so that they would be returned to Earth safely. There are many destined ones here from a variety countries. You see, the Sorcerers of Bairn are blessed at birth to receive an abundance powers. We take a lifetime oath to practice and hone our magical abilities, but we do not achieve our full power until our destined one reaches maturity and appears in our homes. You are very lucky to be my mate. I already have extremely strong powers. You will make me even more powerful."

Garrick walked toward her. His size loomed over her as he approached. "I have been waiting for you since before your birth. I welcome you, Violet, to my home. I hope you will be happy here. You will never return to your old life. Already, your life there has been erased." With a click of his fingers, a window appeared to show the view of Violet's parents standing in mourning clothes next to a newly dug grave. The image ended as it narrowed in to show her mother blowing a kiss toward the casket as it was lowered into the ground. With another click of Garrick's fingers, the picture dissolved.

"It will be your choice to live looking back at your past, or to explore the possibilities that reach into the future." He extended a huge hand toward her, and Violet felt her arm straighten to raise her hand to lay upon his. "It is done," Garrick said ominously, and a lightning bolt of energy jolted down from out of nowhere to surge painfully through their joined hands.

*Khadar*

Instantly tears of agony welled into Violet's eyes. Garrick waved his other hand through the air, and a cooling burst flowed across her burning skin. Holding their hands together, he looked deep into her eyes. "I am glad you are here, Violet. I will take good care of you. I promise." And he caught her gently as she fainted and crumpled to the ground.

Want to read more? One-click The Magic Of Twelve: Violet

## Read more from Pepper North

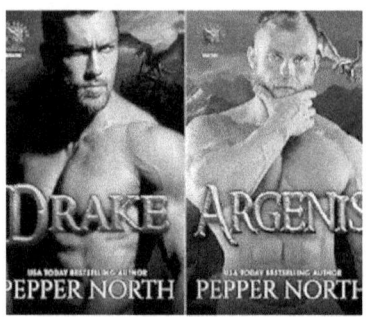

**Fated Dragon Daddies**

Change is coming to Wyvern.
A centuries-old pact between the founders and their powerful allies could save the inhabitants of the city once again, but only a dragon Daddy can truly guard his mate from harm.

*Khadar*

## Shadowridge Guardians

Combining the sizzling talents of bestselling authors Pepper North, Kate Oliver, and Becca Jameson, the Shadowridge Guardians are guaranteed to give you a thrill and leave you dreaming of your own throbbing motorcycle joyride.

Are you daring enough to ride with a club of rough, growly, commanding men? The protective Daddies of the Shadowridge Guardians Motorcycle Club will stop at nothing to ensure the safety and protection of everything that belongs to them: their Littles, their club, and their town. Throw in some sassy, naughty, mischievous women who won't hesitate to serve their fair share of attitude even in the face of looming danger, and this brand new MC Romance series is ready to ignite!

## Danger Bluff

Welcome to Danger Bluff where a mysterious billionaire brings together a hand-selected team of men at an abandoned resort in New Zealand. They each owe him a marker. And they all have something in common–a dominant shared code to nurture and protect. They will repay their debts one by one, finding love along the way.

**A Second Chance For Mr. Right**

For some, there is a second chance at having Mr. Right. Coulda, Shoulda, Woulda explores a world of connections that can't exist... until they do. Forbidden love abounds when these Daddy Doms refuse to live with regret and claim the women who own their hearts.

# Pepper North

## Little Cakes

Welcome to Little Cakes, the bakery that plays Daddy matchmaker! Little Cakes is a sweet and satisfying series, but dare to taste only if you like delicious Daddies, luscious Littles, and guaranteed happily-ever-afters.

### Dr. Richards' Littles®

A beloved age play series that features Littles who find their forever Daddies and Mommies. Dr. Richards guides and supports their efforts to keep their Littles happy and healthy.

Note: Zoey; Dr. Richards' Littles® 1 is available FREE on Pepper's website:
4PepperNorth.club

Dr. Richards' Littles®
is a registered trademark of
With A Wink Publishing, LLC.
All rights reserved.

## SANCTUM

Pepper North introduces you to an age play community that is isolated from the surrounding world. Here Littles can be Little, and Daddies can care for their Littles and keep them protected from the outside world.

## Soldier Daddies

What private mission are these elite soldiers undertaking? They're all searching for their perfect Little girl.

**The Keepers**

This series from Pepper North is a twist on contemporary age play romances. Here are the stories of humans cared for by specially selected Keepers of an alien race. These are science fiction novels that age play readers will love!

**The Magic of Twelve**

The Magic of Twelve features the stories of twelve women transported on their 22nd birthday to a new life as the droblin (cherished Little one) of a Sorcerer of Bairn. These magic wielders have waited a long time to take complete care of their droblin's needs. They will protect their precious one to their last drop of magic from a growing menace. Each novel is a complete story.

# Pepper North

Ever just gone for it? That's what *USA Today* Bestselling Author Pepper North did in 2017 when she posted a book for sale on Amazon without telling anyone. Thanks to her amazing fans, the support of the writing community, Mr. North, and a killer schedule, she has now written more than 80 books!
Enjoy contemporary, paranormal, dark, and erotic romances that are both sweet and steamy? Pepper will convert you into one of her loyal readers. What's coming in the future? A Daddypalooza!

Sign up for Pepper North's newsletter

Like Pepper North on Facebook

Join Pepper's Readers' Group for insider information and giveaways!

Follow Pepper everywhere!
Amazon Author Page
BookBub
FaceBook
GoodReads
Instagram
TikToc
Twitter
YouTube
Visit Pepper's website for a current checklist of books!

www.ingramcontent.com/pod-product-compliance
Lightning Source LLC
LaVergne TN
LVHW021817060526
838201LV00058B/3417